AMATEURS

Books by Donald Barthelme

COME BACK, DR. CALIGARI
SNOW WHITE
UNSPEAKABLE PRACTICES, UNNATURAL ACTS
CITY LIFE
SADNESS
THE DEAD FATHER
AMATEURS

(*For children*)
THE SLIGHTLY IRREGULAR FIRE ENGINE

(*Non-fiction*)
GUILTY PLEASURES

AMATEURS

Donald Barthelme

Routledge & Kegan Paul
London and Henley

First published in Great Britain in 1977
by Routledge & Kegan Paul Ltd,
39 Store Street,
London WC1E 7DD and
Broadway House,
Newtown Road,
Henley-on-Thames,
Oxon RG9 1EN
Printed in Great Britain by
Billing & Sons Limited
Guildford, London and Worcester

"The Great Hug" and *"At the End of the Mechanical Age"* both appeared in
The Atlantic Monthly, *"The Sergeant"* in Fiction, *"And Then"* and
"The Educational Experience" in Harper's Magazine and *"The Reference"*
in Playboy. Except for these six, all the pieces in this book appeared originally
in The New Yorker.

British Library Cataloguing in Publication Data

Barthelme, Donald
Amateurs.
I. Title
823'. 8' 1FS   PS3552.A76

ISBN 0 7100 8742 X

To Grace Paley

Contents

Our Work and Why We Do It   3

The Wound   13

110 West Sixty-first Street   21

Some of Us Had Been Threatening

Our Friend Colby   29

The School   37

The Great Hug   45

I Bought a Little City   51

The Agreement   61

The Sergeant   69

What to Do Next   81

The Captured Woman   89

And Then   105

Porcupines at the University   115

The Educational Experience   125

The Discovery   131

Rebecca   139

CONTENTS

The Reference 147

The New Member 157

You Are as Brave as Vincent van Gogh 167

At the End of the Mechanical Age 175

viii

OUR WORK
AND WHY WE
DO IT

As admirable volume after admirable volume tumbled from the sweating presses . . .

The pressmen wiped their black hands on their pants and adjusted the web, giving it just a little more impression on the right side, where little specks of white had started to appear in the crisp, carefully justified black prose.

I picked up the hammer and said into the telephone, "Well, if he comes around here he's going to get a face full of hammer

"A four-pound hammer can mess up a boy's face pretty bad

"A four-pound hammer can make a bloody rubbish of a boy's face."

I hung up and went into the ink room to see if we had enough ink for the rest of the night's runs.

"Yes, those were weary days," the old printer said with

3

a sigh. "Follow copy even if it flies out the window, we used to say, and oft—"

Just then the Wells Fargo man came in, holding a .38 loosely in his left hand as the manual instructs

It was pointed at the floor, as if he wished to

But then our treasurer, old Claiborne McManus

The knobs of the safe

Sweet were the visions inside.

He handed over the bundle of Alice Cooper T-shirts we had just printed up, and the Wells Fargo man grabbed them with his free hand, gray with experience, and saluted loosely with his elbow, and hurried the precious product out to the glittering fans.

And coming to work today I saw a brown Mercedes with a weeping woman inside, her head was in her hands, a pretty blond back-of-the-neck, the man driving the Mercedes was paying no attention, and

But today we are running the Moxxon Travel Guide in six colors

The problems of makeready, registration, showthrough, and feed

Will the grippers grip the sheet correctly?

And I saw the figure 5 writ in gold

"Down time" was a big factor in the recent negotiations, just as "wash-up time" is expected to complicate the negotiations to come. Percy handed the two-pound can of yellow ink to William.

William was sitting naked in the bed wearing the black hat. Rowena was in the bed too, wearing the red blanket. We have to let them do everything they want to do, because they own the business. Often they scandalize the proofreaders, and then errors don't get corrected and things have to be reset, or additional errors are *inserted* by a proofreader with his mind on the shining thing he has just seen. Atlases are William's special field of interest. There are many places he has never been.

"Yesterday," William began

You have your way of life and we ours

A rush order for matchbook covers for Le Foie de Veau restaurant

The tiny matchbook-cover press is readied, the packing applied, the "Le Foie de Veau" form locked into place. We all stand around a small table watching the matchbook press at work. It is exactly like a toy steam engine. Everyone is very fond of it, although we also have a press big as a destroyer escort—that one has a crew of thirty-five, its own galley, its own sick bay, its own band. We print the currency of Colombia, and the Acts of the Apostles, and the laws of the land, and the fingerprints

"My dancing shoes have rusted," said Rowena, "because I have remained for so long in this bed."

of criminals, and Grand Canyon calendars, and gummed labels, some things that don't make any sense, but that isn't our job, to make sense of things—our job is to kiss the paper with the form or plate, as the case may be, and make sure it's not getting too much ink, and worry about the dot structure of the engravings, or whether a tiny shim is going to work up during the run and split a fountain.

William began slambanging Rowena's dancing shoes with steel wool. "Yesterday," he said

Salesmen were bursting into the room with new orders, each salesman's person bulging with new orders

And old Lucien Frank was pushing great rolls of Luxus Semi-Fine No. 2 through the room with a donkey engine

"Yesterday," William said, "I saw six Sabrett hot-dog

5

stands on wheels marching in single file down the middle of Jane Street followed at a slow trot by a police cruiser. They had yellow-and-blue umbrellas and each hot-dog stand was powered by an elderly man who looked ill. The elderly men not only looked ill but were physically small —not more than five-six, any of them. They were heading I judged for the Sixth Precinct. Had I had the black hat with me, and sufficient men and horses and lariats and .30-.30s, and popular support from the masses and a workable revolutionary ideology and/or a viable myth pattern, I would have rescued them. Removed them to the hills where we would have feasted all night around the fires on tasty Sabrett hot dogs and maybe steaming butts of Ballantine ale, and had bun-splitting contests, sauerkraut-hurling"

He opened the two-pound can of yellow ink with his teeth.

"You are totally wired," Rowena said tenderly

"A boy *likes* to be"

We turned away from this scene, because of what they were about to do, and had some more vodka. Because although we, too, are wired most of the time, it is not the vodka. It is, rather . . . What I mean is, if you have ink in your blood it's hard to get it out of your hands, or to keep your hands off the beautiful typefaces carefully distributed in the huge typecases

Annonce Grotesque
Compacta
Cooper Black
Helvetica Light
Melior
Microgramma Bold
Profil
Ringlet

6

And one of our volumes has just received a scathing notice in *Le Figaro*, which we also print . . . Should we smash the form? But it's *our* form . . .

Old Kermit Dash has just hurt his finger in the paper-cutter. "It's not so bad, Kermit," I said, binding up the wound. "I'm scared of the papercutter myself. Always have been. Don't worry about it. Think instead of the extra pay you will be drawing for that first joint, for the rest of your life. Now get back in there and cut paper." I whacked him on the rump, although he is eighty, almost rumpless

We do the *Oxford Book of American Grub*

Rowena handed Bill another joint—I myself could be interested in her, if she were not part of Management and thus "off limits" to us fiercely loyal artisans. And now, the problem of where to hide the damning statistics in the Doe Airframe Annual Report. Hank Witteborn, our chief designer, suggests that they just be "accidentally left out." The idea has merit, but

Crash! Someone has just thrown something through our biggest window. It is a note with a brick wrapped around it:

> *Sirs:*
> *If you continue to live and breathe*
> *If you persist in walking the path of*
> *Coating the façade of exploitation with*
> *the stucco of good printing*
>
> *Faithfully*

What are they talking about? Was it not we who had the contract for the entire Tanberian Revolution, from the original manifestos hand-set in specially nicked and scarred Blood Gothic to the letterheads of the Office of

7

Permanent Change & Price Control (18 pt. Ultima on a 20-lb. laid stock)? But William held up a hand, and because he was the boss, we let him speak.

"It is good to be a member of the bourgeoisie," he said. "A boy *likes* being a member of the bourgeoisie. Being a member of the bourgeoisie is *good* for a boy. It makes him feel *warm* and *happy*. He can worry about his *plants*. His green plants. His plants and his quiches. His property taxes. The productivity of his workers. His plants/quiches/property taxes/workers/Land Rover. His *sword hilt*. His"

William is sometimes filled with self-hatred, but we are not. We have our exhilarating work, and our motto, "Grow or Die," and our fringe benefits, and our love for William (if only he would take his hands off Rowena's hip bones during business hours, if only he would take off the black hat and put on a pair of pants, a vest, a shirt, socks, and)

I was watching over the imposition of the Detroit telephone book. Someone had just dropped all the H's—a thing that happens sometimes.

"Don't anybody move! Now, everybody bend over and pick up the five slugs nearest him. Now, the next five. Easy does it. Somebody call Damage Control and have them send up extra vodka, lean meat, and bandages. Now, the next five. Anybody that steps on a slug gets the hammer in the mouth. Now, the next"

If only we could confine ourselves to matchbook covers!

But matchbook covers are not our destiny. Our destiny is to accomplish 1.5 million impressions per day. In the next quarter, that figure will be upped by 12 percent, unless

"Leather," William says.

8

"Leather?"

"*Leather*," he says with added emphasis. "Like they cover cows with."

William's next great idea will be in the area of leather. I am glad to know this. His other great ideas have made the company great.

The new machine for printing underground telephone poles

The new machine for printing smoke on smoked hams

The new machine for writing the figure 5 in gold

All of this weakens the heart. I have the hammer, I will smash anybody who threatens, however remotely, the company way of life. We know what we're doing. The vodka ration is generous. Our reputation for excellence is unexcelled, in every part of the world. And will be maintained until the destruction of our art by some other art which is just as good but which, I am happy to say, has not yet been invented.

THE WOUND

He sits up again. He makes a wild grab for his mother's hair. The hair of his mother! But she neatly avoids him. The cook enters with the roast beef. The mother of the torero tastes the sauce, which is presented separately, in a silver dish. She makes a face. The torero, ignoring the roast beef, takes the silver dish from his mother and sips from it, meanwhile maintaining intense eye contact with his mistress. The torero's mistress hands the camera to the torero's mother and reaches for the silver dish. "What is all this nonsense with the dish?" asks the famous aficionado who is sitting by the bedside. The torero offers the aficionado a slice of beef, carved from the roast with a sword, of which there are perhaps a dozen on the bed. "These fellows with their swords, they think they're so fine," says one of the *imbéciles* to another, quietly. The second *imbécil* says, "We would all think ourselves fine if we could. But we can't. Something prevents us."

The torero looks with irritation in the direction of the

imbéciles. His mistress takes the 8-mm. movie camera from his mother and begins to film something outside the window. The torero has been gored in the foot. He is, in addition, surrounded by *imbéciles, idiotas,* and *bobos*. He shifts uncomfortably in his bed. Several swords fall on the floor. A telegram is delivered. The mistress of the torero puts down the camera and removes her shirt. The mother of the torero looks angrily at the *imbéciles*. The famous aficionado reads the telegram aloud. The telegram suggests the torero is a clown and a *cucaracha* for allowing himself to be gored in the foot, thus both insulting the noble profession of which he is such a poor representative and irrevocably ruining the telegram sender's Sunday afternoon, and that, furthermore, the telegram sender is even now on his way to the Church of Our Lady of the Several Sorrows to pray *against* the torero, whose future, he cordially hopes, is a thing of the past. The torero's head flops forward into the cupped hands of an adjacent *bobo*.

The mother of the torero turns on the television set, where the goring of the foot of the torero is being shown first at normal speed, then in exquisite slow motion. The torero's head remains in the cupped hands of the *bobo*. "My foot!" he shouts. Someone turns off the television. The beautiful breasts of the torero's mistress are appreciated by the aficionado, who is also an aficionado of breasts. The *imbéciles* and *idiotas* are afraid to look. So they do not. One *idiota* says to another *idiota*, "I would greatly like some of that roast beef." "But it has not been offered to us," his companion replies, "because we are so insignificant." "But no one else is eating it," the first says. "It simply sits there, on the plate." They regard the attractive roast of beef.

The Wound

The torero's mother picks up the movie camera that his mistress has relinquished and begins filming the torero's foot, playing with the zoom lens. The torero, head still in the hands of the *bobo*, reaches into a drawer in the bedside table and removes from a box there a Cuban cigar of the first quality. Two *bobos* and an *imbécil* rush to light it for him, bumping into each other in the process. "Lysol," says the mother of the torero. "I forgot the application of the Lysol." She puts down the camera and looks around for the Lysol bottle. But the cook has taken it away. The mother of the torero leaves the room, in search of the Lysol bottle. He, the torero, lifts his head and follows her exit. More pain?

His mother reenters the room carrying a bottle of Lysol. The torero places his bandaged foot under a pillow, and both hands, fingers spread wide, on top of the pillow. His mother unscrews the top of the bottle of Lysol. The Bishop of Valencia enters with attendants. The Bishop is a heavy man with his head cocked permanently to the left—the result of years of hearing confessions in a confessional whose right-hand box was said to be inhabited by vipers. The torero's mistress hastily puts on her shirt. The *imbéciles* and *idiotas* retire into the walls. The Bishop extends his hand. The torero kisses the Bishop's ring. The famous aficionado does likewise. The Bishop asks if he may inspect the wound. The torero takes his foot out from under the pillow. The torero's mother unwraps the bandage. There is the foot, swollen almost twice normal size. In the center of the foot, the wound, surrounded by angry flesh. The Bishop shakes his head, closes his eyes, raises his head (on the diagonal), and murmurs a short prayer. Then he opens his eyes and looks about him for a chair. An *idiota* rushes forward with a chair. The Bishop seats

15

himself by the bedside. The torero offers the Bishop some cold roast beef. The Bishop begins to talk about his psychoanalysis: "I am a different man now," the Bishop says. "Gloomier, duller, more fearful. In the name of the Holy Ghost, you would not believe what I see under the bed, in the middle of the night." The Bishop laughs heartily. The torero joins him. The torero's mistress is filming the Bishop. "I was happier with my whiskey," the Bishop says, laughing even harder. The laughter of the Bishop threatens the chair he is sitting in. One *bobo* says to another *bobo,* "The privileged classes can afford psychoanalysis and whiskey. Whereas all we get is sermons and sour wine. This is manifestly unfair. I protest, silently." "It is because we are no good," the second *bobo* says. "It is because we are nothings."

The torero opens a bottle of Chivas Regal. He offers a shot to the Bishop, who graciously accepts, and then pours one for himself. The torero's mother edges toward the bottle of Chivas Regal. The torero's mistress films his mother's surreptitious approach. The Bishop and the torero discuss whiskey and psychoanalysis. The torero's mother has a hand on the neck of the bottle. The torero makes a sudden wild grab for her hair. The hair of his mother! He misses and she scuttles off into a corner of the room, clutching the bottle. The torero picks a killing sword, an *estoque,* from the half dozen still on the bed. The Queen of the Gypsies enters.

The Queen hurries to the torero, little tufts of dried grass falling from her robes as she crosses the room. "Unwrap the wound!" she cries. "The wound, the wound, the wound!" The torero recoils. The Bishop sits severely. His attendants stir and whisper. The torero's mother takes a swig from the Chivas Regal bottle. The famous aficionado

The Wound

crosses himself. The torero's mistress looks down through her half-open blouse at her breasts. The torero quickly reaches into the drawer of the bedside table and removes the cigar box. He takes from the cigar box the ears and tail of a bull he killed, with excellence and emotion, long ago. He spreads them out on the bedcovers, offering them to the Queen. The ears resemble bloody wallets, the tail the hair of some long-dead saint, robbed from a reliquary. "No," the Queen says. She grasps the torero's foot and begins to unwrap the bandages. The torero grimaces but submits. The Queen withdraws from her belt a sharp knife. The torero's mistress picks up a violin and begins to play an air by Valdéz. The Queen whacks off a huge portion of roast beef, which she stuffs into her mouth while bent over the wound—gazing deeply into it, savoring it. Everyone shrinks—the torero, his mother, his mistress, the Bishop, the aficionado, the *imbéciles, idiotas,* and *bobos.* An ecstasy of shrinking. The Queen says, "I want this wound. *This one.* It is mine. Come, pick him up." Everyone present takes a handful of the torero and lifts him high above their heads (he is screaming). But the doorway is suddenly blocked by the figure of an immense black bull. The bull begins to ring, like a telephone.

110 WEST SIXTY-FIRST STREET

Paul gave Eugenie a very large swordfish steak for her birthday. It was wrapped in red-and-white paper. The paper was soaked with swordfish juices in places but Eugenie was grateful nevertheless. He had tried. Paul and Eugenie went to a film. Their baby had just died and they were trying not to think about it. The film left them slightly depressed. The child's body had been given to the hospital for medical experimentation. "But what about life after death?" Eugenie's mother had asked. "There isn't any," Eugenie said. "Are you positive?" her mother asked. "No," Eugenie said. "How can I be positive? But that's my opinion."

Eugenie said to Paul: "This is the best birthday I've ever had." "The hell it is," Paul said. Eugenie cooked the swordfish steak wondering what the hospital had done to Claude. Claude had been two years old when he died. *That goddamn kid!* she thought. Looking around her, she could see the places where he had been—the floor, mostly.

21

Paul thought: My swordfish-steak joke was not successful. He looked at the rather tasteless swordfish on his plate. Eugenie touched him on the shoulder.

Paul and Eugenie went to many erotic films. But the films were not erotic. Nothing was erotic. They began looking at each other and thinking about other people. The back wall of the apartment was falling off. Contractors came to make estimates. A steel I beam would have to be set into the wall to support the floor of the apartment above, which was sagging. The landlord did not wish to pay the four thousand dollars the work would cost. One could see daylight between the back wall and the party wall. Paul and Eugenie went to his father's place in Connecticut for a day. Paul's father was a will lawyer—a lawyer specializing in wills. He showed them a flyer advertising do-it-yourself wills. DO YOU HAVE A WILL? *Everyone should. Save on legal fees—make your own will with Will Forms Kit. Kit has 5 will forms, a 64-page book on wills, a guide to the duties of the executor, and forms for recording family assets. $1.98.* Eugenie studied the third-class mail. "What are our family assets?" she asked Paul. Paul thought about the question. Paul's sister Debbie had had a baby at fifteen, which had been put up for adoption. Then she had become a nun. Paul's brother Steve was in the Secret Service and spent all of his time guarding the widow of a former President. "Does Debbie still believe in a life after death?" Eugenie asked suddenly. "She believes, so far as I can determine, in life *now*," Paul's father said. Eugenie remembered that Paul had told her that his father had been fond, when Debbie was a child, of beating her on her bare buttocks with a dog leash. "She believes in social action," Paul's bent father continued. "Probably she is right. That seems to be the trend among nuns."

Paul thought: Barbados. There we might recover what we have lost. I wonder if there is a charter flight through the Bar Association?

Paul and Eugenie drove back to the city.

"This is a lot of depressing crud that we're going through right now," Paul said as they reached Port Chester, N.Y. "But later it will be better." No it won't, Eugenie thought. "Yes it will," Paul said.

"You are extremely self-righteous," Eugenie said to Paul. "That is the one thing I can't stand in a man. Sometimes I want to scream." "You are a slut without the courage to go out and be one," Paul replied. "Why don't you go to one of those bars and pick up somebody, for God's sake?" "It wouldn't do any good," Eugenie said. "I know that," Paul said. Eugenie remembered the last scene of the erotic film they had seen on her birthday, in which the girl had taken a revolver from a drawer and killed her lover with it. At the time she had thought this a poor way to end the film. Now she wished she had a revolver in a drawer. Paul was afraid of having weapons in the house. "They fire themselves," he always said. "You don't have anything to do with it."

Mason came over and talked. Paul and Mason had been in the army together. Mason, who had wanted to be an actor, now taught speech at a junior college on Long Island. "How are you bearing up?" Mason asked, referring to the death of Claude. "Very well," Paul said. "I am bearing up very well but she is not." Mason looked at Eugenie. "Well, I don't blame her," he said. "She should be an alcoholic by now." Eugenie, who drank very little, smiled at Mason. Paul's jokes were as a rule better than Mason's jokes. But Mason had compassion. His compassion is real, she thought. Only he doesn't know how to express it.

23

Mason told a long story about trivial departmental matters. Paul and Eugenie tried to look interested. Eugenie
had tried to give Claude's clothes to her friend Julia, who
also had a two-year-old. But Julia had said no. "You would
always be seeing them," she said. "You should give them
to a more distant friend. Don't you have any distant
friends?" Paul was promoted. He became a full partner in
his law firm. "This is a big day," he said when he came
home. He was slightly drunk. "There is no such thing as
a big day," Eugenie said. "Once, I thought there was. Now
I know better. I sincerely congratulate you on your pro-
motion, which I really believe was well deserved. You are
talented and you have worked very hard. Forgive me for
that remark I made last month about your self-righteous-
ness. What I said was true—I don't retreat from that
position—but a better wife would have had the tact not to
mention it." "No," Paul said. "You were right to mention
it. It is true. You should tell the truth when you know it.
And you should go out and get laid if you feel like it. The
veneer of politesse we cover ourselves with is not in general good for us." "No," Eugenie said. "Listen. I want to
get pregnant again. You could do that for me. It's probably
a bad idea but I want to do it. In spite of everything." Paul
closed his eyes. "No no no no no," he said.

Eugenie imagined the new child. This time, a girl. A
young woman, she thought, eventually. Someone I could
talk to. With Claude, we made a terrible mistake. We
should have had a small coffin, a grave. We were sensible.
We were unnatural. Paul emerged from the bathroom
with a towel wrapped around his waist. There was some
water on him still. Eugenie touched him on the shoulder.
Paul and Eugenie had once taken a sauna together, in

Norway. Paul had carried a glass of brandy into the sauna and the glass had become so hot that he could not pick it up. The telephone rang. It was Eugenie's sister in California. "We are going to have another child," Eugenie said to her sister. "Are you pregnant?" her sister asked. "Not yet," Eugenie said. "Do you think about him?" her sister asked. "I still see him crawling around on the floor," Eugenie said. "Under the piano. He liked to screw around under the piano."

In the days that followed, Paul discovered a pair of gold cuff links, oval in shape, at the bottom of a drawer. Cuff links, he thought. Could I ever have worn cuff links? In the days that followed, Eugenie met Tiger. Tiger was a black artist who hated white people so much he made love only to white women. "I am color-blind, Tiger," Eugenie said to Tiger, in bed. "I really am." "The hell you are," Tiger said. "You want to run a number on somebody, go ahead. But don't jive *me*." Eugenie admired Tiger's many fine qualities. Tiger "turned her head around," she explained to Paul. Paul tried to remain calm. His increased responsibilities were wearing out his nerve ends. He was guiding a bus line through bankruptcy. Paul asked Eugenie if she was using contraceptives. "Of course," she said.

"How'd it happen?" Tiger asked Eugenie, referring to the death of Claude. Eugenie told him. "That don't make me happy," Tiger said. "Tiger, you are an egocentric mushbrain monster," she said. "You mean I'm a *mean nigger*," Tiger said. He loved to say "nigger" because it shook the white folks so. "I mean you're an imitation wild man. You're about as wild as a can of Campbell's Chicken with Rice soup." Tiger then hit her around the head a few times to persuade her of his authenticity. But she was re-

25

lentless. "When you get right down to it," she said, holding on to him and employing the dialect, "you ain't no better than a *husband.*"

Tiger fell away into the bottomless abyss of the formerly known.

Paul smiled. He had not known it would come to this, but now that it had come to this, he was pleased. The bus line was safely parked in the great garage of Section 112 of the Bankruptcy Act. Time passed. Eugenie's friend Julia came over for coffee and brought her three-year-old son, Peter. Peter walked around looking for his old friend Claude. Eugenie told Julia about the departure of Tiger. "He snorted coke but he would never give me any," she complained. "He said he didn't want to get me started." "You should be grateful," Julia said. "You can't afford it." There was a lot of noise from the back room where workmen were putting in the steel I beam, finally. Paul was promoted from bus-line bankruptcies to railroad bankruptcies. "Today is a big day," he told Eugenie when he got home. "Yes, it is," she said. "They gave me the Cincinnati & West Virginia. The whole thing. It's all mine." "That's wonderful," Eugenie said. "I'll make you a drink." Then they went to bed, he masturbating with long slow strokes, she masturbating with quick light touches, kissing each other passionately all the while.

Paul made more and more money. He bought a boat, a thirty-two-foot Bristol. The sea taught him many things. Bravery descended upon him like sudden rain. Alicia, the new child, stands on the bow wearing a fat orange life jacket. From the shore, lounging waiters at The Captain's Table watch her, wishing her well.

SOME OF US HAD BEEN THREATENING OUR FRIEND COLBY

Some of us had been threatening our friend Colby for a long time, because of the way he had been behaving. And now he'd gone too far, so we decided to hang him. Colby argued that just because he had gone too far (he did not deny that he had gone too far) did not mean that he should be subjected to hanging. Going too far, he said, was something everybody did sometimes. We didn't pay much attention to this argument. We asked him what sort of music he would like played at the hanging. He said he'd think about it but it would take him a while to decide. I pointed out that we'd have to know soon, because Howard, who is a conductor, would have to hire and rehearse the musicians and he couldn't begin until he knew what the music was going to be. Colby said he'd always been fond of Ives's Fourth Symphony. Howard said that this was a "delaying tactic" and that everybody knew that the Ives was almost impossible to perform and would involve weeks of rehearsal, and that the size of the orchestra and chorus would put us way over the music budget. "Be reasonable," he said to Colby. Colby said he'd try to think of something a little less exacting.

Hugh was worried about the wording of the invitations. What if one of them fell into the hands of the authorities? Hanging Colby was doubtless against the law, and if the authorities learned in advance what the plan was they would very likely come in and try to mess everything up. I said that although hanging Colby was almost certainly against the law, we had a perfect *moral* right to do so because he was *our* friend, *belonged* to us in various important senses, and he had after all gone too far. We agreed that the invitations would be worded in such a way that the person invited could not know for sure what he was being invited to. We decided to refer to the event as "An Event Involving Mr. Colby Williams." A handsome script was selected from a catalogue and we picked a cream-colored paper. Magnus said he'd see to having the invitations printed, and wondered whether we should serve drinks. Colby said he thought drinks would be nice but was worried about the expense. We told him kindly that the expense didn't matter, that we were after all his dear friends and if a group of his dear friends couldn't get together and do the thing with a little bit of *éclat*, why, what was the world coming to? Colby asked if he would be able to have drinks, too, before the event. We said, "Certainly."

The next item of business was the gibbet. None of us knew too much about gibbet design, but Tomás, who is an architect, said he'd look it up in old books and draw the plans. The important thing, as far as he recollected, was that the trapdoor function perfectly. He said that just roughly, counting labor and materials, it shouldn't run us more than four hundred dollars. "Good God!" Howard said. He said what was Tomás figuring on, rosewood? No, just a good grade of pine, Tomás said. Victor asked if unpainted pine wouldn't look kind of "raw," and Tomás replied that he thought it could be stained a dark walnut without too much trouble.

I said that although I thought the whole thing ought to be done really well and all, I also thought four hundred dollars for a gibbet, on top of the expense for the drinks, invitations, musicians, and everything, was a bit steep, and why didn't we just use a tree—a nice-looking oak, or something? I pointed out that since it was going to be a June hanging the trees would be in glorious leaf and that not only would a tree add a kind of "natural" feeling but it was also strictly traditional, especially in the West. Tomás, who had been sketching gibbets on the backs of envelopes, reminded us that an outdoor hanging always had to contend with the threat of rain. Victor said he liked the idea of doing it outdoors, possibly on the bank of a river, but noted that we would have to hold it some distance from the city, which presented the problem of getting the guests, musicians, etc., to the site and then back to town.

At this point everybody looked at Harry, who runs a car-and-truck-rental business. Harry said he thought he could round up enough limousines to take care of that end but that the drivers would have to be paid. The drivers, he pointed out, wouldn't be friends of Colby's and couldn't be expected to donate their services, any more than the bartender or the musicians. He said that he had about ten limousines, which he used mostly for funerals, and that he could probably obtain another dozen by calling around to friends of his in the trade. He said also that if we did it outside, in the open air, we'd better figure on a tent or awning of some kind to cover at least the principals and the orchestra, because if the hanging was being rained on he thought it would look kind of dismal. As between gibbet and tree, he said, he had no particular preferences and he really thought that the choice ought to be left up to Colby, since it was his hanging. Colby said that everybody went too far, sometimes, and weren't we being a little Draconian? Howard said rather sharply that all that had already been discussed, and which did he want, gibbet or tree? Colby asked if he could have a firing squad. No, Howard said, he could not. Howard said a firing squad would just be an ego trip for Colby, the blind-fold and last-cigarette bit, and that Colby was in enough hot water already without trying to "upstage" everyone with unnecessary theatrics. Colby said he was sorry, he hadn't meant it that way, he'd take the tree. Tomás crumpled up the gibbet sketches he'd been making, in disgust.

Then the question of the hangman came up. Pete said did we really need a hangman? Because if we used a tree, the noose could be adjusted to the appropriate level and Colby could just jump off something—a chair or stool or something. Besides, Pete said, he very much doubted if there were any free-lance hangmen wandering around the country, now that capital punishment has been done away with absolutely, temporarily, and that we'd probably have to fly one in from England or Spain or one of the South American countries, and even if we did that how could we know in advance that the man was a professional, a real hangman, and not just some money-hungry amateur who might bungle the job and shame us all, in front of everybody? We all agreed then that Colby should just jump off something and that a chair was not what he should jump off of, because that would look, we felt, extremely tacky —some old kitchen chair sitting out there under our beautiful tree. Tomás, who is quite modern in outlook and not afraid of innovation, proposed that Colby be standing on a large round rubber ball ten feet in diameter. This, he said, would afford a sufficient "drop" and would also roll out of the way if Colby suddenly changed his mind after jumping off. He reminded us that by not using a regular hangman we were placing an awful lot of the responsibility for the success of the affair on Colby himself, and that although he was sure Colby would perform creditably and not disgrace his friends at the last minute, still, men have been known to get a little irresolute at times like that, and the ten-foot-round rubber ball, which could probably be fabricated rather cheaply, would insure a "bang-up" production right down to the wire.

At the mention of "wire," Hank, who had been silent all this time, suddenly spoke up and said he wondered if it wouldn't be better if we used wire instead of rope—more efficient and in the end kinder to Colby, he suggested. Colby began looking a little green, and I didn't blame him, because there is something extremely distasteful in thinking about being hanged with wire instead of rope—it gives you sort of a revulsion, when you think about it. I thought it was really quite unpleasant of Hank to be sitting there talking about wire, just when we had solved the problem of what Colby was going to jump off of so neatly, with Tomás's idea about the rubber ball, so I hastily said that wire was out of the question, because it would injure the tree—cut into the branch it was tied to when Colby's full weight hit it—and that in these days of increased respect for the environment, we didn't want that, did we? Colby gave me a grateful look, and the meeting broke up.

Everything went off very smoothly on the day of the event (the music Colby finally picked was standard stuff, Elgar, and it was played very well by Howard and his boys). It didn't rain, the event was well attended, and we didn't run out of Scotch, or anything. The ten-foot rubber ball had been painted a deep green and blended in well with the bucolic setting. The two things I remember best about the whole episode are the grateful look Colby gave me when I said what I said about the wire, and the fact that nobody has ever gone too far again.

THE SCHOOL

Well, we had all these children out planting trees, see, because we figured that . . . that was part of their education, to see how, you know, the root systems . . . and also the sense of responsibility, taking care of things, being individually responsible. You know what I mean. And the trees all died. They were orange trees. I don't know why they died, they just died. Something wrong with the soil possibly or maybe the stuff we got from the nursery wasn't the best. We complained about it. So we've got thirty kids there, each kid had his or her own little tree to plant, and we've got these thirty dead trees. All these kids looking at these little brown sticks, it was depressing.

It wouldn't have been so bad except that just a couple of weeks before the thing with the trees, the snakes all died. But I think that the snakes—well, the reason that the snakes kicked off was that . . . you remember, the boiler was shut off for four days because of the strike, and that was explicable. It was something you could explain

37

to the kids because of the strike. I mean, none of their parents would let them cross the picket line and they knew there was a strike going on and what it meant. So when things got started up again and we found the snakes they weren't too disturbed.

With the herb gardens it was probably a case of over-watering, and at least now they know not to overwater. The children were very conscientious with the herb gardens and some of them probably . . . you know, slipped them a little extra water when we weren't looking. Or maybe . . . well, I don't like to think about sabotage, although it did occur to us. I mean, it was something that crossed our minds. We were thinking that way probably because before that the gerbils had died, and the white mice had died, and the salamander . . . well, now they know not to carry them around in plastic bags.

Of course we *expected* the tropical fish to die, that was no surprise. Those numbers, you look at them crooked and they're belly-up on the surface. But the lesson plan called for a tropical-fish input at that point, there was nothing we could do, it happens every year, you just have to hurry past it.

We weren't even supposed to have a puppy.

We weren't even supposed to have one, it was just a puppy the Murdoch girl found under a Gristede's truck one day and she was afraid the truck would run over it when the driver had finished making his delivery, so she stuck it in her knapsack and brought it to school with her. So we had this puppy. As soon as I saw the puppy I thought, Oh Christ, I bet it will live for about two weeks and then . . . And that's what it did. It wasn't supposed to be in the classroom at all, there's some kind of regula-tion about it, but you can't tell them they can't have a

The School

puppy when the puppy is already there, right in front of them, running around on the floor and yap yap yapping. They named it Edgar—that is, they named it after me. They had a lot of fun running after it and yelling, "Here, Edgar! Nice Edgar!" Then they'd laugh like hell. They enjoyed the ambiguity. I enjoyed it myself. I don't mind being kidded. They made a little house for it in the supply closet and all that. I don't know what it died of. Distemper, I guess. It probably hadn't had any shots. I got it out of there before the kids got to school. I checked the supply closet each morning, routinely, because I knew what was going to happen. I gave it to the custodian.

And then there was this Korean orphan that the class adopted through the Help the Children program, all the kids brought in a quarter a month, that was the idea. It was an unfortunate thing, the kid's name was Kim and maybe we adopted him too late or something. The cause of death was not stated in the letter we got, they suggested we adopt another child instead and sent us some interesting case histories, but we didn't have the heart. The class took it pretty hard, they began (I think; nobody ever said anything to me directly) to feel that maybe there was something wrong with the school. But I don't think there's anything wrong with the school, particularly, I've seen better and I've seen worse. It was just a run of bad luck. We had an extraordinary number of parents passing away, for instance. There were I think two heart attacks and two suicides, one drowning, and four killed together in a car accident. One stroke. And we had the usual heavy mortality rate among the grandparents, or maybe it was heavier this year, it seemed so. And finally the tragedy.

The tragedy occurred when Matthew Wein and Tony Mavrogordo were playing over where they're excavating for the new federal office building. There were all these big wooden beams stacked, you know, at the edge of the excavation. There's a court case coming out of that, the parents are claiming that the beams were poorly stacked. I don't know what's true and what's not. It's been a strange year.

I forgot to mention Billy Brandt's father, who was knifed fatally when he grappled with a masked intruder in his home.

One day, we had a discussion in class. They asked me, where did they go? The trees, the salamander, the tropical fish, Edgar, the poppas and mommas, Matthew and Tony, where did they go? And I said, I don't know, I don't know. And they said, who knows? and I said, nobody knows. And they said, is death that which gives meaning to life? and I said, no, life is that which gives meaning to life. Then they said, but isn't death, considered as a fundamental datum, the means by which the taken-for-granted mundanity of the everyday may be transcended in the direction of—

I said, yes, maybe.

They said, we don't like it.

I said, that's sound.

They said, it's a bloody shame!

I said, it is.

They said, will you make love now with Helen (our teaching assistant) so that we can see how it is done? We know you like Helen.

I do like Helen but I said that I would not.

We've heard so much about it, they said, but we've never seen it.

I said I would be fired and that it was never, or almost

40

never, done as a demonstration. Helen looked out of the window.

They said, please, please make love with Helen, we require an assertion of value, we are frightened.

I said that they shouldn't be frightened (although I am often frightened) and that there was value everywhere. Helen came and embraced me. I kissed her a few times on the brow. We held each other. The children were excited. Then there was a knock on the door, I opened the door, and the new gerbil walked in. The children cheered wildly.

THE GREAT HUG

At the last breakfast after I told her, we had steak and eggs. Bloody Marys. Three pieces of toast. She couldn't cry, she tried. Balloon Man came. He photographed the event. He created the Balloon of the Last Breakfast After I Told Her—a butter-colored balloon. "This is the kind of thing I do so well," he said. Balloon Man is not modest. No one has ever suggested that. "This balloon is going to be extra-famous and acceptable, a documentation of raw human riches, the plain canvas gravy of the thing. The Pin Lady will never be able to bust this balloon, never, not even if she hugs me for a hundred years." We were happy to have pleased him, to have contributed to his career.

The Balloon Man won't sell to kids.

Kids will come up to the Balloon Man and say, "Give us a blue balloon, Balloon Man," and the Balloon Man will say, "Get outa here kids, these balloons are adults-only." And the kids will say, "C'mon, Balloon Man, give us a red balloon and a green balloon and a white balloon, we got the money." "Don't want any kid-money," the Balloon Man will say, "kid-money is wet and nasty and makes your hands wet and nasty and then you wipe 'em on your pants and your pants get all wet and nasty and you sit down to eat and the *chair* gets all wet and nasty, let that man in the brown hat draw near, he wants a balloon." And the kids will say, "Oh please Balloon Man, we want five yellow balloons that never pop, we want to make us a smithereen." "Ain't gonna make no smithereen outa my fine yellow balloons," says the Balloon Man, "your red balloon will pop sooner and your green balloon will pop later but your yellow balloon will never pop no matter how you stomp on it or stick it and besides the Balloon Man don't sell to kids, it's against his principles."

The Balloon Man won't let you take his picture. He has something to hide. He's a superheavy Balloon Man, doesn't want the others to steal his moves. It's all in the gesture—the precise, reunpremeditated right move.

Balloon Man sells the Balloon of Fatigue and the Balloon of Ora Pro Nobis and the Rune Balloon and the Balloon of the Last Thing to Do at Night; these are saffron-, cinnamon-, salt-, and celery-colored, respectively. He sells the Balloon of Not Yet and the Balloon of Sometimes. He works the circus, every circus. Some people don't go to the circus and so don't meet the Balloon Man and don't get to buy a balloon. That's sad. Near to most people in any given city at any given time won't be at the circus. That's unfortunate. They don't get to buy a brown, whole-life-long cherishable Sir Isaiah Berlin Balloon. "I don't sell the Balloon Jejune," the Balloon Man will say, "let them other people sell it, let them other people have all that wet and nasty kid-money mitosising in their sock. That a camera you got there mister? Get away." Balloon

Man sells the Balloon of Those Things I Should Have Done I Did Not Do, a beige balloon. And the Balloon of the Ballade of the Crazy Junta, crimson of course. Balloon Man stands in a light rain near the popcorn pushing the Balloon of Wish I Was, the Balloon of Busoni Thinking, the Balloon of the Perforated Septum, the Balloon of Not Nice. Which one is my balloon, Balloon Man? Is it the Balloon of the Cartel of Noose Makers? Is it the Balloon of God Knows I Tried?

One day the Balloon Man will meet the Pin Lady. It's in the cards, in the stars, in the entrails of sacred animals. Pin Lady is a woman with pins stuck in her couture, rows of pins and pins not in rows but placed irregularly here a pin there a pin, maybe eight thousand pins stuck in her couture or maybe ten thousand pins or twelve thousand pins. Pin Lady tells the truth. The embrace of Balloon Man and Pin Lady will be something to see. They'll roll down the hill together, someday. Balloon Man's arms will be wrapped around Pin Lady's pins and Pin Lady's embrangle will be wrapped around Balloon Man's balloons— even the yellow balloons. They'll roll down the hill together. Pin Lady has the Pin of I Violently Desire. She has the Pin of Crossed Fingers Behind My Back, she has the Pin of Soft Talk, she has the Pin of No More and she is rumored to have the Pin of the Dazed Sachem's Last Request. She's into puncture. When puncture becomes widely accepted and praised, it will be the women who will have the sole license to perform it, Pin Lady says.

Pin Lady has the Pin of Tomorrow Night—a wicked pin, those who have seen it say. That great hug, when Balloon Man and Pin Lady roll down the hill together, will be frightening. The horses will run away in all directions. Ordinary people will cover their heads with shopping bags. I don't want to think about it. You blow up all them balloons yourself, Balloon Man? Or did you have help? Pin Lady, how come you're so apricklededee? Was it something in your childhood?

Balloon Man will lead off with the Balloon of Grace Under Pressure, Do Not Pierce or Incinerate.

Pin Lady will counter with the Pin of Oh My, I Forgot.

Balloon Man will produce the Balloon of Almost Wonderful. Pin Lady will come back with the Pin of They Didn't Like Me Much. Balloon Man will sneak in there with the Balloon of the Last Exit Before the Toll Is Taken. Pin Lady will reply with the Pin of One Never Knows for Sure. Balloon Man will propose the Balloon of Better Days. Pin Lady, the Pin of Whiter Wine.

It's gonna be *bad,* I don't want to think about it.

Pin Lady tells the truth. Balloon Man doesn't lie, exactly. How can the Quibbling Balloon be called a lie? Pin Lady is more straightforward. Balloon Man is less straightforward. Their stances are semiantireprophetical. They're falling down the hill together, two falls out of three. Pin him, Pin Lady. Expand, Balloon Man. When he created our butter-colored balloon, we felt better. A little better. The event that had happened to us went floating out into the world, was made useful to others. Balloon Man says, "I got here the Balloon of the Last Concert. It's not a bad balloon. Some people won't like it. Some people *will* like it. I got the Balloon of Too Terrible. Not every balloon can make you happy. Not every balloon can trigger glee. *But I insist that these balloons have a right to be heard!* Let that man in the black cloak step closer, he wants a balloon.

"The Balloon of Perhaps. My best balloon."

I BOUGHT
A LITTLE
CITY

So I bought a little city (it was Galveston, Texas) and told everybody that nobody had to move, we were going to do it just gradually, very relaxed, no big changes overnight. They were pleased and suspicious. I walked down to the harbor where there were cotton warehouses and fish markets and all sorts of installations having to do with the spread of petroleum throughout the Free World, and I thought, A few apple trees here might be nice. Then I walked out this broad boulevard which has all these tall thick palm trees maybe forty feet high in the center and oleanders on both sides, it runs for blocks and blocks and ends up opening up to the broad Gulf of Mexico—stately homes on both sides and a big Catholic church that looks more like a mosque and the Bishop's Palace and a handsome red brick affair where the Shriners meet. I thought, What a nice little city, it suits me fine.

It suited me fine so I started to change it. But softly, softly. I asked some folks to move out of a whole city block on I Street, and then I tore down their houses. I put the people into the Galvez Hotel, which is the nicest hotel in town, right on the seawall, and I made sure that every room had a beautiful view. Those people had wanted to stay at the Galvez Hotel all their lives and never had a chance before because they didn't have the money. They were delighted. I tore down their houses and made that empty block a park. We planted it all to hell and put some nice green iron benches in it and a little fountain—all standard stuff, we didn't try to be imaginative.

I was pleased. All the people who lived in the four blocks surrounding the empty block had something they hadn't had before, a park. They could sit in it, and like that. I went and watched them sitting in it. There was already a black man there playing bongo drums. I hate bongo drums. I started to tell him to stop playing those goddamn bongo drums but then I said to myself, No, that's not right. You got to let him play his goddamn bongo drums if he feels like it, it's part of the misery of democracy, to which I subscribe. Then I started thinking about new housing for the people I had displaced, they couldn't stay in that fancy hotel forever.

But I didn't have any ideas about new housing, except that it shouldn't be too imaginative. So I got to talking to one of these people, one of the ones we had moved out, guy by the name of Bill Caulfield who worked in a whole-sale-tobacco place down on Mechanic Street.

"So what kind of a place would you like to live in?" I asked him.

"Well," he said, "not too big."

"Uh-huh."

"Maybe with a veranda around three sides," he said, "so we could sit on it and look out. A screened porch, maybe."

"Whatcha going to look out at?"

"Maybe some trees and, you know, the lawn."

"So you want some ground around the house."

"That would be nice, yeah."

" 'Bout how much ground are you thinking of?"

"Well, not too much."

"You see, the problem is, there's only x amount of ground and everybody's going to want to have it to look at and at the same time they don't want to be staring at the neighbors. Private looking, that's the thing."

"Well, yes," he said. "I'd like it to be kind of private."

"Well," I said, "get a pencil and let's see what we can work out."

We started with what there was going to be to look at, which was damned difficult. Because when you look you don't want to be able to look at just one thing, you want to be able to shift your gaze. You need to be able to look at at least three things, maybe four. Bill Caulfield solved the problem. He showed me a box. I opened it up and inside was a jigsaw puzzle with a picture of the Mona Lisa on it.

"Lookee here," he said. "If each piece of ground was like a piece of this-here puzzle, and the tree line on each piece of property followed the outline of a piece of the puzzle—well, there you have it, Q.E.D. and that's all she wrote."

"Fine," I said. "Where are the folk going to park their cars?"

"In the vast underground parking facility," he said.

"O.K., but how does each householder gain access to his household?"

"The tree lines are double and shade beautifully paved walkways possibly bordered with begonias," he said.

"A lurkway for potential muggists and rapers," I pointed out.

53

"There won't be any such," Caulfield said, "because you've bought our whole city and won't allow that class of person to hang out here no more."

That was right. I had bought the whole city and could probably do that. I had forgotten.

"Well," I said finally, "let's give 'er a try. The only thing I don't like about it is that it seems a little imaginative."

We did and it didn't work out badly. There was only one complaint. A man named A. G. Bartie came to see me.

"Listen," he said, his eyes either gleaming or burning, I couldn't tell which, it was a cloudy day, "I feel like I'm living in this gigantic jiveass jigsaw puzzle."

He was right. Seen from the air, he was living in the middle of a titanic reproduction of the Mona Lisa, too, but I thought it best not to mention that. We allowed him to square off his property into a standard 60 x 100 foot lot and later some other people did that too—some people just like rectangles, I guess. I must say it improved the concept. You run across an occasional rectangle in Shady Oaks (we didn't want to call the development anything too imaginative) and it surprises you. That's nice.

I said to myself:

> Got a little city
> Ain't it pretty

By now I had exercised my proprietorship so lightly and if I do say so myself tactfully that I wondered if I was enjoying myself enough (and I had paid a heavy penny too—near to half my fortune). So I went out on the streets then and shot six thousand dogs. This gave me great satisfaction and you have no idea how wonderfully it improved

54

the city for the better. This left us with a dog population of 165,000, as opposed to a human population of something like 89,000. Then I went down to the Galveston *News,* the morning paper, and wrote an editorial denouncing myself as the vilest creature the good God had ever placed upon the earth, and were we, the citizens of this fine community, who were after all free Americans of whatever race or creed, going to sit still while one man, *one man,* if indeed so vile a critter could be so called, etc. etc.? I gave it to the city desk and told them I wanted it on the front page in fourteen-point type, boxed. I did this just in case they might have hesitated to do it themselves, and because I'd seen that Orson Welles picture where the guy writes a nasty notice about his own wife's terrible singing, which I always thought was pretty decent of him, from some points of view.

A man whose dog I'd shot came to see me.

"You shot Butch," he said.

"Butch? Which one was Butch?"

"One brown ear and one white ear," he said. "Very friendly."

"Mister," I said, "I've just shot six thousand dogs, and you expect me to remember Butch?"

"Butch was all Nancy and me had," he said. "We never had no children."

"Well, I'm sorry about that," I said, "but I own this city."

"I know that," he said.

"I am the sole owner and I make all the rules."

"They told me," he said.

"I'm sorry about Butch but he got in the way of the big campaign. You ought to have had him on a leash."

"I don't deny it," he said.

"You ought to have had him inside the house."

"He was just a poor animal that had to go out sometimes."

"And mess up the streets something awful?"

"Well," he said, "it's a problem. I just wanted to tell you how I feel."

"You didn't tell me," I said. "How do you feel?"

"I feel like bustin' your head," he said, and showed me a short length of pipe he had brought along for the purpose.

"But of course if you do that you're going to get your ass in a lot of trouble," I said.

"I realize that."

"It would make you feel better, but then I own the jail and the judge and the po-lice and the local chapter of the American Civil Liberties Union. All mine. I could hit you with a writ of mandamus."

"You wouldn't do that."

"I've been known to do worse."

"You're a black-hearted man," he said. "I guess that's it. You'll roast in Hell in the eternal flames and there will be no mercy or cooling drafts from any quarter."

He went away happy with this explanation. I was happy to be a black-hearted man in his mind if that would satisfy the issue between us because that was a bad-looking piece of pipe he had there and I was still six thousand dogs ahead of the game, in a sense. So I owned this little city which was very, very pretty and I couldn't think of any more new innovations just then or none that wouldn't get me punctuated like the late Huey P. Long, former governor of Louisiana. The thing is, I had fallen in love with Sam Hong's wife. I had wandered into this store on Tremont Street where they sold Oriental novelties, paper lanterns, and cheap china and bamboo birdcages and wicker footstools and all that kind of thing. She was smaller than I was and I thought I had never seen that much goodness in a woman's face before. It was hard to credit. It was the best face I'd ever seen.

"I can't do that," she said, "because I am married to Sam."

"Sam?"

She pointed over to the cash register where there was a Chinese man, young and intelligent-looking and pouring that intelligent look at me with considered unfriendliness.

"Well, that's dismal news," I said. "Tell me, do you love me?"

"A little bit," she said, "but Sam is wise and kind and we have one and one-third lovely children."

She didn't look pregnant but I congratulated her anyhow, and then went out on the street and found a cop and sent him down to H Street to get me a bucket of Colonel Sanders' Kentucky Fried Chicken, extra crispy. I did that just out of meanness. He was humiliated but he had no choice. I thought:

> I own a little city
> Awful pretty
> Can't help people
> Can hurt them though
> Shoot their dogs
> Mess 'em up
> Be imaginative
> Plant trees
> Best to leave 'em alone?
> Who decides?
> Sam's wife is Sam's wife and coveting
> Is not nice.

So I ate the Colonel Sanders' Kentucky Fried Chicken, extra crispy, and sold Galveston, Texas, back to the interests. I took a bath on that deal, there's no denying it, but I learned something—don't play God. A lot of other people already knew that, but I have never doubted for a minute that a lot of other people are smarter than me, and figure things out quicker, and have grace and statistical norms on their side. Probably I went wrong by being too imaginative, although really I was guarding against that. I did very little, I was fairly restrained. God does a lot worse things, every day, in one little family, any family, than I did in that whole little city. But He's got a better imagination than I do. For instance, I still covet Sam Hong's wife. That's torment. Still covet Sam Hong's wife, and probably always will. It's like having a tooth pulled. For a year. The same tooth. That's a sample of His imagination. It's powerful.

So what happened? What happened was that I took the other half of my fortune and went to Galena Park, Texas, and lived inconspicuously there, and when they asked me to run for the school board I said No, I don't have any children.

THE AGREEMENT

Where is my daughter?

Why is she there? What crucial error did I make? Was there more than one?

Why have I assigned myself a task that is beyond my abilities?

Having assigned myself a task that is beyond my abilities, why do I then pursue it with all of the enthusiasm of one who believes himself capable of completing the task?

Having assigned myself a task that is beyond my abilities, why do I then do that which is most certain to preclude my completing the task? To ensure failure? To excuse failure? Ordinary fear of failure?

When I characterize the task as beyond my abilities, do I secretly believe that it is within my powers?

Was there only one crucial error, or was there a still more serious error earlier, one that I did not recognize as such at the time?

Was there a series of errors?

Are they in any sense forgivable? If so, who is empowered to forgive me?

If I fail in the task that is beyond my abilities, will my lover laugh?

Will the mailman laugh? The butcher?

When will the mailman bring me a letter from my daughter?

Why do I think my daughter might be dead or injured when I know that she is almost certainly well and happy? If I fail in the task that is beyond my abilities, will my daughter's mother laugh?

But what if the bell rings and I go down the stairs and answer the door and find there an old woman with white hair wearing a bright-red dress, and when I open the door she immediately begins spitting blood, a darker red down the front of her bright-red dress?

If I fail in the task that is beyond my abilities, will my doctor laugh?

Why do I conceal from my doctor what it is necessary for him to know?

Is my lover's lover a man or a woman?

Will my father and mother laugh? Are they already laughing, secretly, behind their hands?

If I succeed in the task that is beyond my abilities, will I win the approval of society? If I win the approval of society, does this mean that the (probable) series of errors already mentioned will be forgiven, or, if not forgiven, viewed in a more sympathetic light? Will my daughter then be returned to me?

Will I deceive myself about the task that is beyond my abilities, telling myself that I have successfully completed it when I have not?

Will others aid in the deception?

Will others unveil the deception?

But what if the bell rings and I go down the stairs and answer the door and find there an old man with white hair wearing a bright-red dress, and when I open the door he immediately begins spitting blood, a darker red down the front of his bright-red dress?

Why did I assign myself the task that is beyond my abilities?

Did I invent my lover's lover or is he or she real? Ought I to care?

But what if the bell rings and I go down the stairs again and instead of the white-haired woman or man in the bright-red dress my lover's lover is standing there? And what if I bring my lover's lover into the house and sit him or her down in the brown leather club chair and provide him or her with a drink and begin to explain that the task I have undertaken is hopelessly, hopelessly beyond my abilities? And what if my lover's lover listens with the utmost consideration, nodding and smiling and patting my wrist at intervals as one does with a nervous client, if one is a lawyer or doctor, and then abruptly offers me a new strategy: Why not do *this*? And what if, thinking over the new strategy proposed by my lover's lover, I recognize that yes, *this* is the solution which has evaded me for these many months? And what if, recognizing that my lover's lover has found the solution which has evaded me for these many months, I suddenly begin spitting blood, dark red against the blue of my blue work shirt? What then?

For is it not the case that even with the solution in hand, the task will remain beyond my abilities?

And where is my daughter? What is my daughter thinking at this moment? Is my daughter, at this moment, being knocked off her bicycle by a truck with the words HACHARD & CIE painted on its sides? Or is she, rather, in a photographer's studio, sitting for a portrait I have requested? Or has she already done so, and will, today, the bell ring and the mailman bring a large stiff brown envelope stamped PHOTO DO NOT BEND?

HACHARD & CIE?
PHOTO DO NOT BEND?

If I am outraged and there is no basis in law or equity for my outrage nor redress in law or equity for my outrage, am I to decide that my outrage is wholly inappropriate? If I observe myself carefully, using the techniques of introspection most favored by society, and decide, after such observation, that my outrage is not wholly inappropriate but perhaps partially appropriate, what can I do with my (partially appropriate) outrage? What is there to do with it but deliver it to my lover or my lover's lover or to the task that is beyond my abilities, or to embrace instead the proposition that, after all, things are not so bad? Which is not true?

If I embrace the proposition that, after all, things are not so bad, which is not true, then have I not also embraced a hundred other propositions, kin to the first in that they are also not true? That the Lord is my shepherd, for example?

But what if I decide not to be outraged but to be, instead, calm and sensible? Calm and sensible and adult? And mature? What if I decide to send my daughter stamps for her stamp collection and funny postcards and birthday and Christmas packages and to visit her at the

times stated in the agreement? And what if I assign myself simpler, easier tasks, tasks which are well within my
powers? And what if I decide that my lover has no other
lover (disregarding the matchbooks, the explanations
that do not explain, the discrepancies of time and place),
and what if I inform my doctor fully and precisely about
my case, supplying all relevant details (especially the
shameful)? And what if I am able to redefine my errors
as positive adjustments to a state of affairs requiring
positive adjustments? And what if the operator does *not*
break into my telephone conversation, any conversation,
and say, "I'm sorry, this is the operator, I have an emer-
gency message for 679–9819"?

Will others aid in the deception?

Will others unveil the deception?

"TWELFTH: Except for the obligations, promises and
agreements herein set forth and to be performed by the
husband and wife respectively, and for rights, obligations
and causes of action arising out of or under this agreement, all of which are expressly reserved, the husband and
wife each hereby, for himself or herself and for his or her
legal representatives, forever releases and discharges the
other, and the heirs and legal representatives of the other,
from any and all debts, sums of money, accounts, con-
tracts, claims, cause or causes of action, suits, dues,
reckonings, bills, specialties, covenants, controversies,
agreements, promises, variances, trespasses, damages,
judgments, extents, executions and demands, whatso-
ever, in law or in equity, which he or she had, or has or
hereafter can, shall or may have, by reason of any matter,
from the beginning of the world to the execution of this
agreement."

The painters are here. They are painting the apartment. One gallon of paint to eight gallons of benzine. From the beginning of the world to the execution of this agreement. Where is my daughter? I am asking for a carrot to put in the stone soup. The villagers are hostile.

THE SERGEANT

The orderly looked at the paper and said, There's nothing wrong with this. Take it to room 400.

I said, Wait a minute.

The orderly looked at me. I said, Room 400.

I said something about a lawyer.

He got to his feet. You know what that is? he asked, pointing to an M.P. in the hall.

I said yes, I remembered.

O.K. Room 400. Take this with you.

He handed me the paper.

I thought, They'll figure it out sooner or later. And: The doctor will tell them.

The doctor said, Hello, young trooper.

•

The other sergeant looked at me. How come you made sergeant so quick?

I was always a sergeant, I said. I was a sergeant the last time, too.

I got more time in grade, he said, so I outrank you.

I said not if you figured from my original date-of-rank which was sometime in '53.

Fifty-three, he said, what war was that?

I said the war with the Koreans.

I heard about it, he said. But you been away a long time.

I said that was true.

What we got here is a bunch of re-cruits, he said, they don't love the army much.

I said I though⁺ they were all volunteers.

The e-conomic debacle volunteered 'em, he said, they heard the eagle shits once a month regularly.

I said nothing. His name was Tomgold.

They'll be rolling training grenades under your bunk, he said, just as soon as we teach 'em how to pull the pin.

I said they wouldn't do that to me because I wasn't sup-posed to be here anyway, that it was all a mistake, that I'd done all this before, that probably my discharge papers would come through any day now.

That's right, he said, you do look kind of old. Can you still screw?

•

I flicked on the barracks lights.

All right you men, I said.

But there was only one. He sat up in his bunk wearing skivvies, blinking in the light.

O.K. soldier roll out.

The Sergeant

What time is it sarge?

It's five-forty-five soldier, get dressed and come with me. Where are the other men?

Probably haven't got back from town, sarge.

They have overnight passes?

Always got passes, sarge. Lots and lots of passes. Look, I got a pass too.

He showed me a piece of paper.

You want me to write you a pass, sarge?

I said I really wasn't supposed to be here at all, that I'd done all this before, that it was all a mistake.

You want me to fix you up with discharge papers, sarge? It'll cost you.

I said that if his section chief found out what he was doing they'd put him way back in the jailhouse.

You want me to cut some orders for you, sarge? You want a nice TDY to Hawaii?

I said I didn't want to get mixed up in anything.

If you're mixed up in this, then you got to get mixed up in that, he said. Would you turn them lights out, as you go?

•

The I.G. was a bird colonel with a jumper's badge and a general's pistol belt. He said, Well, sergeant, all I know is what's on the paper.

Yes, sir, I said, but couldn't you check it out with the records center?

They're going to have the same piece of paper I have, sergeant.

I said that I had been overseas for sixteen months during the Korean War and that I had then been reassigned to Fort Lewis, Washington, where my C.O. had been a Captain Llewellyn.

None of this is in your 201 file, the I.G. said.

Maybe there's somebody else with my name.

Your name *and* your serial number?

Colonel, I did all this before. Twenty years ago.

You don't look that old, sergeant.

I'm forty-two.

Not according to this.

But that's wrong.

The colonel giggled. If you were a horse we could look at your teeth.

Yes, sir.

O.K. sergeant I'll take it under advisement.

Thank you, sir.

I sat on the edge of my bed and looked at my two pairs of boots beautifully polished for inspection, my row of shirts hanging in my cubicle with all the shoulder patches facing the same way.

I thought: Of course, it's what I deserve. I don't deny that. Not for a minute.

•

Sergeant, he said, I'd be greatly obliged.

I said I wasn't sure I had fifty dollars to lend.

Look in your pocket there, sargie, the lieutenant said. Or maybe you have a bank account?

I said yes but not here.

72

The Sergeant

My momma is sick and I need fifty dollars to take the bus home, he said. You don't want to impede my journey in the direction of my sick momma, do you?

What has she got? I asked.

Who?

Your mother.

I'll let you keep my 'lectric frying pan as security, the lieutenant said, showing it to me.

I'm not supposed to be in the army at all, I said. It's a fuckup of some kind.

Where are you from, sargie-san? You can cook yourself the dishes of your home region, in this frying pan.

I said the food in the NCO mess was pretty good, considering.

You're not going to lend me the fifty dollars?

I didn't say that, I said.

Sergeant, I can't *order* you to lend me the fifty dollars.

I know that, sir.

It's against regulations to do that, sergeant.

Yes, sir.

I can't read and write, sergeant.

You can't read and write?

If they find out, my ass is in terrible, terrible trouble, sergeant.

Not at all?

You want a golf club? I'll sell you a golf club. Fifty dollars.

I said I didn't play.

What about my poor momma, sergeant?

I said I was sorry.

I ride the blue bus, sergeant. Carries me clear to Gainesville. You ever ride the blue bus, sergeant?

•

I spoke to the chaplain who was playing the pinball machine at the PX. I said I didn't love the army much.

Nonsense, the chaplain said, you do, you do, you do or you wouldn't be here. Each of us is where we are, sergeant, because we want to be where we are and because God wants us to be where we are. Everybody in life is in the right place, believe me, may not seem that way sometimes but take it from me, take it from me, all part of the Divine plan, you got any quarters on you?

I gave him three quarters I had in my pocket.

Thank you, he said, I'm in the right place, you're in the right place, what makes you think you're so different from me? You think God doesn't know what He's doing? I'm right here ministering to the Screaming Falcons of the Thirty-third Division and if God didn't want me to be ministering to the wants and needs of the Screaming Falcons of the Thirty-third Division I wouldn't be here, would I? What makes you think you're so different from me? Works is what counts, boy, forget about anything else and look to your works, your works tell the story, nothing wrong with you, three stripes and two rockers, you're doing very well, now leave me, leave me, don't let me see your face again, you hear, sergeant? Good boy.

I thought: Works?

•

Two M.P.'s stopped me at the main gate.
Where you headed, sergeant?

The Sergeant

I said I was going home.

That's nice, said the taller of the two. You got any orders?

I showed them a pass.

How come you takin' off at this hour, sergeant? It's four o'clock in the morning. Where's your car?

I said I didn't have a car, thought I'd walk to town and catch a bus.

The M.P.'s looked at me peculiarly.

In this fog and stuff? they asked.

I said I liked to walk in the early morning.

Where's your gear, sergeant? Where's your A.W.O.L. bag? You don't have a bag?

I reached into the pocket of my field jacket and showed them my razor and a fresh T-shirt.

What's your outfit, sergeant?

I told them.

The shorter M.P. said: But this razor's not clean.

We all crowded closer to look at the razor. It was not clean.

And this-here pass, he said, it's signed by General Zachary Taylor. Didn't he die?

•

I was holding on to a sort of balcony or shelf that had been tacked on to the third floor of the barracks. It was about to fall off the barracks and I couldn't get inside because somebody'd nailed the windows shut.

Hey, slick, came a voice from the parking lot, you gonna fall.

75

Yes yes, I said, I'm going to fall.

Jump down here, she said, and I'll show you the secrets of what's under my shirt.

Yeah yeah, I said, I've heard that before.

Jump little honey baby, she said, you won't regret it.

It's so far, I said.

Won't do nothin' 'cept break your head, she called, at the very worst.

I don't want my head broken, I said, trying to get my fingers into that soft decayed pine.

Come on, G.I., she said, you ain't comfortable up there.

I did all this, I said, once, twenty years ago. Why do I have to do it all over again?

You do look kind of old, she said, you an R.A. or something? Come down, my little viper, come down.

I either jumped or did not jump.

•

I thought: Of course, it's what I deserve. I don't deny it for a minute.

The captain said: Harm that man over there, sergeant.

Yes, sir. Which one?

The one in the red tie.

You want me to harm him?

Yes, with your M-16.

The man in the red tie. Blue suit.

Right. Go ahead. Fire.

Black shoes.

That's the one, sergeant, are you temporizing?

I think he's a civilian, sir.

You're refusing an order, sergeant?

The Sergeant

No I'm not refusing sir I just don't think I can do it.

Fire your weapon sergeant.

He's not even in uniform, sir, he's wearing a suit. And he's not doing anything, he's just standing there.

You're refusing a direct order?

I just don't feel up to it, sir. I feel weak.

Well sergeant if you don't want to harm the man in the red tie I'll give you an alternative. You can stuff olives with little onions for the general's martinis.

That's the alternative?

There are eight hundred thousand gallon cans of olives over at the general's mess, sergeant. And four hundred thousand gallon cans of little onions. I think you ought to consider that.

I'm allergic to onions, sir. They make me break out. Terribly.

Well you've a nice little problem there, haven't you, sergeant? I'll give you thirty seconds.

•

The general was wearing a white short-sleeved shirt, blue seersucker trousers, and gold wire-rimmed glasses.

Four olives this time, sergeant.

I said: Andromache!

WHAT TO DO NEXT

So.

The situation is, I agree, desperate. But fortunately I know the proper way to proceed. That is why I am giving you these instructions. They will save your life. First, persuade yourself that the situation is not desperate (my instructions will save your life only if you have not already hopelessly compromised it by listening to the instructions of others, or to the whispers of your heart, which is in itself suspect, in that it has been taught how to behave—how to whisper, even—by the very culture that has produced the desperate situation). Persuade yourself, I say, that your original perception of the situation was damaged by not having taken into account all of the variables (for example, my instructions) and that the imminent disaster that hangs in the sky above you can be, with justice, downgraded to the rank of severe inconvenience by the application of corrected thinking. Do not let what happened to the dog weaken your resolve.

Yes, the dog is dead, I admit it. I'm sorry. I admit also that putting eight-foot-square paintings of him in every room of the house has not consoled you. But, studying the paintings, you will notice after a time that in each painting the artist has included, in the background, or up in the left-hand corner, not only your dog but other dogs, dogs not known to you—perhaps dogs that were formerly friends of your dog but that you did not know he knew. Thus the whole concept "other dog" suddenly thrusts itself into your consciousness, and looking more intently now at those strange spaniels, retrievers, terriers, you understand that one of them, or one very much like one of them, might just possibly become the "new dog"—the "new dog" of which you have been, until now, afraid to think. For life must go on, after all, and that you have been able to think *new dog* is already a victory, of a kind, for the instructions.

Next, write your will. I know that you are too young to take this step, or at least this is what you have always told yourself, when will-writing time rolled around; this time, do it. Leave everything to your wife, if you have one; or to your old school, if you have one. This prudent action, which you would not have taken had it not been for the instructions, implies nothing about your future health and well-being. Don't worry. Next, see your Loan Officer, and borrow a sizable sum to leave to people, for what good is a will if it does not have the strong arm of hard cash to implement it with? You are tidying up, yes, but do not permit this kind of activity to frighten you. Lose yourself in the song of the instructions, in the precise, detailed balm of having had solved for you that most difficult of problems, what to do next.

Now, housecleaning. It is true that what she is saying doesn't interest you very much, but don't tell her (or, if you are a woman, him—the instructions are flexible, the instructions do not discriminate). Smile. Smile and tell her that the two of you have come to "the end of the line" —she is interesting but false. (It is not true that she is interesting but it is true that she is false.) Your true love lies elsewhere, and always will. I know that it's depressing, this maneuver (she has hung her shirt in your closet, and now you must give it back) but your life is more important than any of these merely temporal alignments, which give you someone to sleep with, yes, but on the other hand require a lot of smiling—smiling that you cannot spare, if you are to turn a smiling face and a ready, acquiescent nod to the just demands of the instructions. There! The thing is done. Lead her, weeping, from the closet, the green garment you never liked much dangling from one hand, and put her on a bus. Goodbye, Elsie.

I know that you are depressed, but pay attention: the instructions have arranged a diversion for you. Sea air! Passage has been booked in your name to Hong Kong on the *Black Swan*, the *Black Tulip*, or the *Tanta Maru*. Running away from trouble is always an excellent partial solution, but we anticipate using this tactic only temporarily, until other measures, still being honed and polished (there you are in the crew's mess, drinking anisette with Rudi and Hans, the crew members who have befriended you, and listening to their stories about waves, to which you respond a shade too enthusiastically, like those people, usually English, one finds at a jazz place overenjoying the music, their mouths open too ecstatically, their fingerpopping too Anglo-Saxon), are ready for presentation to the green breast of the New World. You need not thank the instructions just yet; they have not completed their designs, although they are pleased that *you* are pleased with the life of the forecastle, which you would never have tasted in all its saltiness had it not been for them.

Quickly now, avoid that other sticky development that is developing on the left, a hazard you would not have identified had it not been for the sage wisdom of the instructions, which anticipate everything, even their own blind spots, of which they possess not a few. The instructions are, for example, blind to the blandishments of the soft life, which other sets of instructions uphold, cultivate, make possible. But that life is not for you, you do not have the panache to carry it off. You are in fact a rather poor specimen, in some ways, and entering a fashionable hotel in Bern with a vastly beautiful woman on your arm, her thin skeleton curling toward you, and forty or fifty pieces of good luggage following, you would only look ridiculous. Where did you purchase those trousers? Trousers made out of old rugs have not been *haut monde* for two years. Remember Elsie. Forget Zoë. Stop plucking nervously at your rugs. Pay attention.

Because we are ready to move toward the center of your difficulties, which is the fact that you are no good. This great handicap, which many of our best people have labored under, is irrevocable. This is the nut of your dilemma, and to crack it you must proceed in the following way (remember that you still have a new dog to buy, and a true love to fail to find, and while we are at it we have been thinking about certain alterations that need to be made on your house—a wall torn out here, a soffit to be plastered there, the plumber summoned to make the drains drain, all crucial to giving your leaning personality the definition that it lamentably lacks). The instructions, at this point, call for a rewriting of your fundamental documents through useful work. Many considerations now intrude. Your former employment as a pilot project for A.A., although possessed of some degree of social worth, does not, in our analysis, finally qualify. It stressed your objecthood, your existence as vessel, your flasklike qualities, and neglected, to our mind, the creative potentialities you might contain. We have thought about possible alternatives. The Bengal Lancers are no longer recruiting. I.B.M. is a very large company but all of the good jobs are already taken. Your love of life would seem to equip you for a role on "Love of Life," but, we have discovered, others, similarly equipped, have got there ahead of you. There is a chief's rating open on the *Tanta Maru* and a cook's on the *Black Tulip*, but these have been filled by Rudi and Hans, who have asked to be remembered to you. You could become a dog painter in the tradition of Landseer, but there are already seventy thousand of these in New York City alone—leadership in that field is not easily come by.

Starting fresh, as it is called, requires that you know the appropriate corn and rain dances, but also that you can stand the terrific wrenches of the spirit that accompany frontier-busting, as it is called. When you change your life, you also break your back (or have an equivalent serious illness) within the next twelve months—that is a statistically sound statement. But the instructions will protect you, more or less, from these hazards (and it would not surprise me if, at this point, you wondered aloud why the instructions are being so kind to you, specifically you; the answer is simple, you have taken the trouble to read them). The culture that we share, such as it is, makes of us all either machines for assimilating and judging that culture, or uncritical sops who simply sop it up, become it. Clearly it is better to be the first than the second, or at least that is our provisional judgment, at this time. Because you stick out from the matrix of this culture like a banged thumb, swelling and reddening and otherwise irrupting all over its smooth, eventless surface, our effort must be to contain you, as would, for example, a lead glove. (Note your movement from container, which you were in your former life, before you renewed yourself, with the aid of the instructions, to contained, the latter a much more active principle, lively and wroth-causing—another success story for the cunning and gay instructions, which, although they may seem to you a shade self-congratulatory and vain, are in truth only *right*.) We have therefore decided to make you *a part of the instructions themselves*—something other people must complete, or go through, before they reach their individual niches, or thrones, or whatever kind of plateau makes them, at least for the time being, happy. Thus, we have specified that everyone who comes to us from this day forward must take twelve hours of you a week, for which they will receive three points credit per semester, and, as well, a silver spoon in the "Heritage" pattern. Don't hang back. We are sure you are up to it. Many famous teachers teach courses in themselves; why should you be different, just because you are a wimp and a lame, objectively speaking? Courage. The anthology of yourself which will be used as a text is even now being assembled by underpaid researchers in our textbook division, drawing upon the remembrances of those who hated you and those (a much smaller number) who loved you. You will be adequate in your new role. See? Your life is saved. The instructions do not make distinctions between those lives which are worth saving and those which are not. Your life is saved. Congratulations. I'm sorry.

THE CAPTURED WOMAN

The captured woman asks if I will take her picture.

I shoot four rolls of 35 mm. and then go off very happily to the darkroom . . .

I bring back the contacts and we go over them together. She circles half a dozen with a grease pencil—pictures of herself staring. She does not circle pictures of herself smiling, although there are several very good ones. When I bring her back prints (still wet) she says they are not big enough.

"Not big enough?"

"Can you make enlargements?"

"How big?"

"How big can you make them?"

"The largest paper I have is 24 by 36."

"Good!"

The very large prints are hung around her room with pushpins.

"Make more."

"For what?"

"I want them in the other rooms too."

"The staring ones?"

"Whichever ones you wish."

I make more prints using the smiling negatives. (I also shoot another half dozen rolls.) Soon the house is full of her portraits, she is everywhere.

•

M. calls to tell me that he has captured a woman too.

"What kind?"

"Thai. From Thailand."

"Can she speak English?"

"Beautifully. She's an English teacher back home, she says."

"How tall?"

"As tall as yours. Maybe a little taller."

"What is she doing?"

"Right now?"

"Yes."

"She's polishing her rings. I gave her a lot of rings. Five rings."

"Was she pleased?"

"I think so. She's polishing like a house afire. Do you think that means she's tidy?"

"Have to wait and see. Mine is throwing her football."

"What?"

"I gave her a football. She's sports-minded. She's throwing passes into a garbage can."

"Doesn't that get the football dirty?"

"Not the regular garbage can. I got her a special garbage can."

"Is she good at it?"

"She's good at *everything*."

There was a pause.

"Mine plays the flute," M. says. "She's asked for a flute."

"Mine probably plays the flute too but I haven't asked her. The subject hasn't come up."

"Poor Q.," M. says.

"Oh, come now. No use pitying Q."

"Q. hasn't a chance in the world," M. says, and hangs up.

•

I say: "What will you write in the note?"

"You may read it if you wish. I can't stop you. It's you after all who will put it in the mail."

"Do you agree not to tell him where you are?"

"This is going to be almost impossible to explain. You understand that."

"Do you love him?"

"I waited six years to have a baby."

"What does that mean?"

"I wasn't sure, I suppose."

"Now you're sure?"

"I was growing older."

"How old are you now?"

"Thirty-two last August."

"You look younger."

"No I don't."

She is tall and has long dark hair which has, in truth, some gray in it already.

She says: "You were drunk as a lord the first time I saw you."

"Yes, I was."

When I first met her (in a perfectly ordinary social situation, a cocktail party) she clutched my wrists, tapping them then finally grabbing, in the wildest and most agitated way, meanwhile talking calmly about some movie or other.

She's a wonderful woman, I think.

•

She wants to go to church!

"What!"

"It's Sunday."

"I haven't been inside a church in twenty years. Except in Europe. Cathedrals."

"I want to go to church."

"What kind?"

"Presbyterian."

"Are you a Presbyterian?"

"I was once."

I find a Presbyterian church in the Yellow Pages.

We sit side by side in the pew for all the world like a married couple. She is wearing a beige linen suit which modulates her body into a nice safe Sunday quietude.

The two ministers have high carved chairs on either side of the lectern. They take turns conducting the service. One is young, one is old. There is a choir behind us and a solo tenor so startlingly good that I turn my head to look at him.

We stand and sit and sing with the others as the little mimeographed order-of-service dictates.

The old minister, fragile, eagle beak, white close-cropped hair, stands at the lectern in a black cassock and white thin lacy surplice.

"*Sacrifice,*" the minister says.

He stares into the choir loft for a moment and then repeats the thought: "Sacrifice."

We are given a quite admirable sermon on Sacrifice which includes quotations from Euripides and A. E. Housman.

After the service we drive home and I tie her up again.

•

It is true that Q. will never get one. His way of proceeding is far too clumsy. He might as well be creeping about carrying a burlap sack.

P. uses tranquillizing darts delivered by a device which resembles the Sunday *New York Times.*

D. uses chess but of course this limits his field of operations somewhat.

S. uses a spell inherited from his great-grandmother.

F. uses his illness.

T. uses a lasso. He can make a twenty-foot loop and keep it spinning while he jumps in and out of it in his handmade hundred-and-fifty-dollar boots—a mesmerizing procedure.

C. has been accused of jacklighting, against the law in

this state in regard to deer. The law says nothing about women.

X. uses the Dionysiac frenzy.

L. is the master. He has four now, I believe.

I use Jack Daniel's.

•

I stand beside one of the "staring" portraits and consider whether I should attempt to steam open the note.

Probably it is an entirely conventional appeal for rescue.

I decide that I would rather not know what is inside, and put it in the mail along with the telephone bill and a small ($25) contribution to a lost but worthy cause.

•

Do we sleep together? Yes.

What is to be said about this?

It is the least strange aspect of our temporary life together. It is as ordinary as bread.

She tells me what and how. I am sometimes inspired and in those moments need no instructions. Once I made an X with masking tape at a place on the floor where we'd made love. She laughed when she saw it. That is, I am sometimes able to amuse her.

What does she think? Of course, I don't know. Perhaps she regards this as a parenthesis in her "real" life, like a stay in the hospital or being a member of a jury sequestered in a Holiday Inn during a murder trial. I have criminally abducted her and am thus clearly in the wrong, a circumstance which enables her to regard me very kindly.

She is a wonderful woman and knows herself to be wonderful—she is (justifiably) a little vain.

The rope is forty feet long (that is, she can move freely forty feet in any direction) and is in fact thread—Belding mercerized cotton, shade 1443.

What does she think of me? Yesterday she rushed at me and stabbed me three times viciously in the belly with a book, the Viking *Portable Milton*. Later I visited her in her room and was warmly received. She let me watch her doing her exercises. Each exercise has a name and by now I know all the names: Boomerang, Melon, Hip Bounce, Diamond, Whip, Hug, Headlights, Ups and Downs, Bridge, Flags, Sitting Twist, Swan, Bow and Arrow, Turtle, Pyramid, Bouncing Ball, Accordion. The movements are amazingly erotic. I knelt by her side and touched her lightly. She smiled and said, not now. I went to my room and watched television—*The Wide World of Sports*, a soccer match in São Paulo.

•

The captured woman is smoking her pipe. It has a long graceful curving stem and a white porcelain bowl decorated with little red flowers. For dinner we had shad roe and buttered yellow beans.

"He looks like he has five umbrellas stuck up his ass," she says suddenly.

"Who?"

"My husband. But he's a very decent man. But of course

95

that's not uncommon. A great many people are very decent. Most people, I think. Even you."

The fragrance of her special (ladies' mixture) tobacco hangs about us.

"This is all rather like a movie. That's not a criticism. I like things that are like movies."

I become a little irritated. All this effort and all she can think of is movies?

"This is not a movie."

"It is," she says. "It is it is it is."

•

M. calls in great agitation.

"Mine is sick," he says.

"What's the matter?"

"I don't know. She's listless. Won't eat. Won't polish. Won't play her flute."

M.'s is a no-ass woman of great style and not inconsiderable beauty.

"She's languishing," I say.

"Yes."

"That's not good."

"No."

I pretend to think—M. likes to have his predicaments taken seriously.

"Speak to her. Say this: My soul is soused, imparadised, imprisoned in my lady."

"Where's that from?"

"It's a quotation. Very powerful."

"I'll try it. Soused, imprisoned, imparadised."

"No. Imparadised, imprisoned. It actually sounds better

the way you said it, though. Imparadised last."

"O.K. I'll say it that way. Thanks. I love mine more than you love yours."

"No you don't."

"Yes I do."

I bit off my thumb, and bade him do as much.

•

The extremely slow mailman brings her an answer to her note.

I watch as she opens the envelope.

"That bastard," she says.

"What does he say?"

"That incredible bastard."

"What?"

"I offer him the chance to rescue me on a white horse—one of the truly great moments this life affords—and he natters on about how well he and the kid are doing together. How she hardly ever cries now. How *calm* the house is."

"The bastard," I say happily.

"I can see him sitting in the kitchen by the microwave oven and reading his *Rolling Stone*."

"Does he read *Rolling Stone*?"

"He thinks *Rolling Stone* is neat."

"Well . . ."

"He's not *supposed* to be reading *Rolling Stone*. It's not aimed at him. He's too old, the dumb fuck."

"You're angry."

"Damn right."

"What are you going to do?"

She thinks for a moment.

"What happened to your hand?" she says, noticing at last.

"Nothing," I say, placing the bandaged hand behind my back. (Obviously I did not bite the thumb clean through but I did give it a very considerable gnaw.)

"Take me to my room and tie me up," she says. "I'm going to hate him for a while."

I return her to her room and go back to my own room and settle down with *The Wide World of Sports*—international fencing trials in Belgrade.

•

This morning, at the breakfast table, a fierce attack from the captured woman.

I am a shit, a vain preener, a watcher of television, a blatherer, a creephead, a monstrous coward who preys upon etc. etc. etc. and is not man enough to etc. etc. etc. Also I drink too much.

This is all absolutely true. I have often thought the same things myself, especially, for some reason, upon awakening.

I have a little more Canadian bacon.

"And a skulker," she says with relish. "One who—"

I fix her in the view finder of my Pentax and shoot a whole new series, *Fierce*.

The trouble with capturing one is that the original gesture is almost impossible to equal or improve upon.

•

She says: "He wants to get that kid away from me. He wants to keep that kid for himself. He has captured that kid."

"She'll be there when you get back. Believe me."

"When will that be?"

"It's up to you. You decide."

"Ugh."

Why can't I marry one and live with her uneasily ever after? I've tried that.

"Take my picture again."

"I've taken enough pictures. I don't want to take any more pictures."

"Then I'll go on Tuesday."

"Tuesday. O.K. That's tomorrow."

"Tuesday is tomorrow?"

"Right."

"Oh."

She grips the football and pretends to be about to throw it through the window.

"Do you ever capture somebody again after you've captured them once?"

"Almost unheard of."

"Why not?"

"It doesn't happen."

"Why not?"

"It just doesn't."

"Tomorrow. Oh my."

I go into the kitchen and begin washing the dishes— the more scutwork you do, the kindlier the light in which you are regarded, I have learned.

•

I enter her room. L. is standing there.

"What happened to your hand?" he asks.

"Nothing," I say.

Everyone looks at my bandaged hand for a moment—not long enough.

"Have you captured her?" I ask.

L. is the master, the nonpareil, the O. J. Simpson of our aberration.

"I have captured him," she says.

"Wait a minute. That's not how it works."

"I changed the rules," she says. "I will be happy to give you a copy of the new rules which I have written out here on this legal pad."

L. is smirking like a mink, obviously very pleased to have been captured by such a fine woman.

"But wait a minute," I say. "It's not Tuesday yet!"

"I don't care," she says. She is smiling. At L.

I go into the kitchen and begin scrubbing the oven with Easy-Off.

How original of her to change the rules! She is indeed a rare spirit.

"French Russian Roquefort or oil-and-vinegar," she says sometimes, in her sleep—I deduce that she has done some waitressing in her day.

•

The captured woman does a backward somersault from a standing position.

I applaud madly. My thumb hurts.

"Where is L.?"

"I sent him away."

"Why?"

"He had no interesting problems. Also he did a sketch of me which I didn't like."

She shows me the charcoal sketch (L.'s facility is famous) and it is true that her beauty suffers just a bit, in this sketch. He must have been spooked a little by my photographs, which he did not surpass.

"Poor L."

The captured woman does another somersault. I applaud again. Is today Tuesday or Wednesday? I can't remember.

"Wednesday," she says. "Wednesday the kid goes to dance after which she usually spends the night with her pal Regina because Regina lives close to dance. So there's really no point in my going back on a Wednesday."

•

A week later she is still with me. She is departing by degrees.

If I tore her hair out, no one but me would love her. But she doesn't want me to tear her hair out.

I wear different shirts for her: red, orange, silver. We hold hands through the night.

AND THEN

The part of the story that came next was suddenly missing, I couldn't think of it, so I went into the next room and
drank a glass of water (my "and then" still hanging in the
frangible air) as if this were the most natural thing in the
world to do at that point, thinking that I would "make up"
something, while in the other room, to put in place of that
part of the anecdote that had fallen out of my mind, to
keep the light glittering in his cautious eyes. And in truth
I was getting a little angry with him now, not fiercely
angry but slightly *désabusé,* because he had been standing very close to me, closer than I really like people to
stand, the rims of his shoes touching the rims of my
shoes, our belt buckles not four inches distant, a com-
pletely unwarranted impingement upon my personal
space. And so I went, as I say, into the next room and
drank a glass of water, trying to remember who he was
and why I was talking to him, not that he wasn't friendly,
if by "friendly" you mean standing aggressively close to

people with an attentive air and smiling teeth, that's not what I mean by "friendly," and it was right then that I decided to lie to him, although what I had been telling him previously was true, to the best of my knowledge and belief. But, faced now with this "gap" in the story, I decided to offer him a good-quality lie in place of the part I couldn't remember, a better strategy, I felt, than simply stopping, leaving him with a maimed, not-whole anecdote, violating his basic trust, simple faith, or personhood even, for all I knew. But the lie had to be a good one, because if your lie is badly done it makes everyone feel wretched, liar and lied-to alike plunged into the deepest lackadaisy, and everyone just feels like going into the other room and drinking a glass of water, or whatever is available there, whereas if you can lie really well then you get dynamite results, 35 percent report increased intellectual understanding, awareness, insight, 40 percent report more tolerance, acceptance of others, liking for self, 29 percent report they receive more personal and more confidential information from people and that others become more warm and supportive toward them—all in consequence of a finely orchestrated, carefully developed untruth. And while I was thinking about this, counting my options, I noticed that he was a policeman, had in fact a dark-blue uniform, black shoes, a badge and a gun, a policeman's hat, and I noticed also that my testicles were aching, as they sometimes do if you sit too long in an uncomfortable or strained position, but I had been standing, and then I understood, in a flash, that what he wanted from me was not to hear the "next" part of my story, or anecdote, but that I give my harpsichord to his wife as a present.

And Then

Now, my harpsichord has been out of tune for five years, some of the keys don't function, and there are drink rings on top of it where people have set their drinks down carelessly, at parties and the like, still it is mine and I didn't particularly want to give it to his wife, I believe her name is Cynthia, and although I may have drunkenly promised to give it to her in a fit of generosity or inadvertence, or undue respect for the possible pleasures of distant others, still it was and is my harpsichord and what was his wife giving me? I hadn't in mind sexual favors or anything of that kind, I had in mind real property of equivalent value. So I went into the other room and drank a glass of water, or rather vodka, thinking to stall him with the missing "part" of the trivial anecdote I had been telling him, to keep his mind off what he wanted, the harpsichord, but the problem was, what kind of lie would he like? I could tell him about "the time I went to Hyde Park for a drink with the President," but he could look at me and know I was too young to have done that, and then the failed lie would exist between us like a bathtub filled with ruinous impotent nonsense, he would simply seize the harpsichord and make off with it (did I say that he was a sergeant? with three light-blue chevrons sewn to the darker blue of his right and left sleeves?). Who knows the kinds of lies that sergeants like, something that would confirm their already existing life-attitudes, I supposed, and I tried to check back mentally and remember what these last might be, drawing upon my (very slight) knowledge of the sociology of authority, something in the area of child abuse perhaps, if I could fit a child-abuse part to the structure already extant, which I was beginning to forget, something to do with

walking at night, if I could spot-weld a child-abuse exten-
sion to what was already there, my partial anecdote, that
might do the trick.

So I went into the next room and had a glass of something, I think I said, "Excuse me," but maybe I didn't, and
it had to be a fabrication that would grammatically follow the words "and then" without too much of a seam
showing, of course I could always, upon reentering the
first room, where the sergeant stood, begin the sentence
anew, with some horrific instance of child abuse, of which
I have several in the old memory bank, and we could
agree that it was terrible, terrible, what people did, and
he would forget about the harpsichord, and we could part
with mutual regard, generated by the fact (indisputable)
that neither of us were child abusers, however much we
might have liked to be, having children of our own. Or, to
get away from the distasteful subject of hurting children,
I might tack, to the flawed corpus of the original anecdote,
something about walking at night in the city, a declara-
tion of my own lack of leftness—there's not a radical
bone in my body, all I want is ease and bliss, not a thing
in this world do I desire other than ease and bliss, I think
he might empathize with that (did I mention that he had
the flap on his holster unbuttoned and his left hand resting on the butt of his weapon, and the rim of his black
shoes touching the rim of my brown boots?). That might
ring a bell.

Or I could, as if struck by a sudden thought, ask him
if he was a "real" policeman. He would probably answer
truthfully. He would probably say either, "Yes, I am a real
policeman," or, "No, I am not a real policeman." A third
possibility: "What do you mean by 'real,' in this instance?"
Because even among policemen who are "real," that is,

bona fide, duly appointed officers of the law, there are degrees of realness and vivacity, they say of one another, "Fred's a *real* policeman," or announce a finding contrary to this finding, I don't know this of my own knowledge but am extrapolating from my knowledge (very slight) of the cant of other professions. But if I asked him this question, as a dodge or subterfuge to cover up the fact of the missing "part" of the original, extremely uninteresting, anecdote, there would be an excellent chance that he would take umbrage, and that his colleagues (did I neglect to say that there are two of his colleagues, in uniform, holding on to the handles of their bicycles, standing behind him, stalwartly, in the other room, and that he himself, the sergeant, is holding on to the handle of his bicycle, stalwartly, with the hand that is not resting on the butt of his .38, teak-handled I believe, from the brief glance that I snuck at it, when I was in the other room?) would take umbrage also. Goals incapable of attainment have driven many a man to despair, but despair is easier to get to than that—one need merely look out of the window, for example. But what we are trying to do is to get away from despair and over to ease and bliss, and that can never be attained with three policemen, with bicycles, standing alertly in your other room. They can, as we know, make our lives more miserable than they are already if we arouse their ire, which must be kept slumbering, by telling them stories, for example, such as the story of the four bears, known to us all from childhood (although not everyone knows about the fourth bear) and it is clear that *they can't lay their bicycles down* and sit, which would be the normal thing, no, they must stand there at more-or-less parade rest, some departmental ruling that I don't know about, but of course it irritates them, it even irritates me, and I am not standing there holding up a bicycle, I am in the other room having a glass of beef broth with a twist of lemon, perhaps you don't believe me about the policemen but there they are, pictures lie but words don't, unless one is lying on purpose, with an end in view, such as to get three policemen with bicycles out of your other room while retaining your harpsichord (probably the departmental regulations state that the bicycles must never be laid down in a civilian space, such as my other room, probably the sergeant brought his colleagues to help him haul away the harpsichord, which has three legs, and although the sight of three policemen on bicycles, each holding aloft one leg of a harpsichord, rolling smoothly through the garment district, might seem ludicrous to you, who knows how it seems to them? entirely right and proper, no doubt) which he, the sergeant, considers I promised to his wife as a wedding present, and it is true that I was at the wedding, but only to raise my voice and object when the minister came to that part of the ceremony where he routinely asks for objections, *"Yes!"* I shouted, *"she's my mother! And although she is a widow, and legally free, she belongs to me in dreams!"* but I was quickly hushed up by a quartet of plainclothesmen, and the ceremony proceeded. But what is the good of a mother if she is another man's wife, as they mostly are, and not around in the morning to fix your buckwheat cakes or Rice Krispies, as the case may be, and in the evening to argue with you about your vegetables, and in the middle of the day to iron your shirts and clean up your rooms, and at all times to provide intimations of ease and bliss (however misleading and ill-founded), but instead insists on hauling your harpsichord away (did I note that Mother, too, is in the other room,

with the three policemen, she is standing with the top
half of her bent over the instrument, her arms around it,
at its widest point—the keyboard end)? So, standing with
the glass in my hand, the glass of herb tea with sour
cream in it, I wondered what kind of useful prosthesis I
could attach to the original anecdote I was telling all
these people in my other room—those who seem so satisfied with their tableau, the three peelers posing with their
bicycles, my mother hugging the harpsichord with a
mother's strangle—what kind of "and then" I could con-
trive which might satisfy all the particulars of the case,
which might redeliver to me my mother, retain to me my
harpsichord, and rid me of these others, in their uniforms.

I could tell them the story of the (indeterminate number of) bears, twisting it a bit to fit my deeper designs, so
that the fourth bear enters (from left) and says, "I don't
care who's been sleeping in my bed just so long as it is
not a sergeant of police," and the fifth bear comes in
(from right) and says, "Harpsichords wither and warp
when their soundboards are exposed to the stress of bicycle transport," and the sixth bear strides right down to
the footlights, center stage (from a hole in the back of
the theater, or a hole in the back of the anecdote), and
says, "Dearly beloved upholders, enforcers, rush, rush
away and enter the six-year bicycle race that is even now
awaiting the starter's gun at the corner of Elsewhere and
Not-Here," and the seventh bear descends from the flies
on a nylon rope and cries, *Mother! Come home!* and the
eighth bear—

But bears are not the answer. Bears are for children.
Why am I thinking about bears when I should be thinking
about some horribly beautiful "way out" of this tense
scene, which has reduced me to a rag, just contemplating

it here in the other room with this glass of chicken livers *flambé* in my hand—

Wait.

I will reenter the first room, cheerfully, confidently, even gaily, and throw chicken livers *flambé* all over the predicament, the flaming chicken livers clinging like incindergel to Mother, policemen, bicycles, harpsichord, and my file of the *National Review* from its founding to the present time. That will "open up" the situation successfully. I will resolve these terrible contradictions with flaming chicken parts and then sing the song of how I contrived the ruin of my anaconda.

PORCUPINES
AT THE
UNIVERSITY

"And now the purple dust of twilight time/ steals across the meadows of my heart," the Dean said.

His pretty wife, Paula, extended her long graceful hands full of Negronis.

A scout burst into the room, through the door. "Porcupines!" he shouted.

"Porcupines what?" the Dean asked.

"Thousands and thousands of them. Three miles down the road and comin' fast!"

"Maybe they won't enroll," the Dean said. "Maybe they're just passing through."

"You can't be sure," his wife said.

"How do they look?" he asked the scout, who was pulling porcupine quills out of his ankles.

"Well, you know. Like porcupines."

"Are you going to bust them?" Paula asked.

"I'm tired of busting people," the Dean said.

"They're not people," Paula pointed out.

"De bustibus non est disputandum," the scout said.

"I suppose I'll have to do something," the Dean said.

•

Meanwhile the porcupine wrangler was wrangling the porcupines across the dusty and overbuilt West.

Dust clouds. Yips. The lowing of porcupines.

"Git along theah li'l porcupines."

And when I reach the great porcupine canneries of the East, I will be rich, the wrangler reflected. I will sit on the front porch of the Muehlebach Hotel in New York City and smoke me a big seegar. Then, the fancy women.

"All right you porcupines step up to that yellow line."

There was no yellow line. This was just an expression the wrangler used to keep the porcupines moving. He had heard it in the army. The damn-fool porcupines didn't know the difference.

The wrangler ambled along reading the ads in a copy of *Song Hits* magazine. PLAY HARMONICA IN 5 MINS. and so forth.

The porcupines scuffled along making their little hops. There were four-five thousand in the herd. Nobody had counted exactly.

An assistant wrangler rode in from the outskirts of the herd. He too had a copy of *Song Hits* magazine, in his hip pocket. He looked at the head wrangler's arm, which had a lot of little holes in it.

"Hey Griswold."

"Yeah?"

"How'd you get all them little holes in your arm?"

"You ever try to slap a brand on a porky-pine?"

Probably the fancy women will be covered with low-cut dresses and cheap perfume, the wrangler thought. Probably there will be hundreds of them, hundreds and hundreds. All after my medicine bundle containing my gold and my lucky drill bit. But if they try to rush me I will pull out my guitar. And sing them a song of prairie virility.

•

"Porcupines at the university," the Dean's wife said. "Well, why not?"

"We don't have *facilities* for four or five thousand porcupines," the Dean said. "I can't get a dial tone."

"They could take Alternate Life Styles," Paula said.

"We've already got too many people in Alternate Life Styles," the Dean said, putting down the telephone. "The hell with it. I'll bust them myself. Single-handed. Ly."

"You'll get hurt."

"Nonsense, they're only porcupines. I'd better wear my old clothes."

"Bag of dirty shirts in the closet," Paula said.

The Dean went into the closet.

Bags and bags of dirty shirts.

"Why doesn't she ever take these shirts to the laundry?"

•

Griswold, the wrangler, wrote a new song in the saddle.

Fancy woman fancy woman
How come you don't do right

117

I oughta rap you in the mouth for the way you acted
In the porte cochère of the Trinity River Consolidated
General High last Friday
   Nite.

I will sit back and watch it climbing the charts, he said
to himself. As recorded by Merle Travis. First, it will be a
Bell Ringer. Then, the Top Forty. Finally a Golden Oldie.
   "All right you porcupines. Git along."
   The herd was moving down a twelve-lane trail of silky-
smooth concrete. Signs along the trail said things like
NEXT EXIT 5 MI. and RADAR IN USE.
   "Griswold, some of them motorists behind us is gettin'
awful pissed."
   "I'm runnin' this-here porky-pine drive," Griswold said,
"and I say we better gettum off the road."
   The herd was turned onto a broad field of green grass.
Green grass with white lime lines on it at ten-yard in-
tervals.
   The Sonny and Cher show, the wrangler thought. Well,
Sonny, how I come to write this song, I was on a porky-
pine drive. The last of the great porky-pine drives you
might say. We had four-five thousand head we'd fatted
up along the Tuscalora and we was headin' for New York
City.

•

   The Dean loaded a gleaming Gatling gun capable of delivering 360 rounds a minute. The Gatling gun sat in a
mule-drawn wagon and was covered with an old piece

of canvas. Formerly it had sat on a concrete slab in front of the ROTC Building.

First, the Dean said to himself, all they see is this funky old wagon pulled by this busted-up old mule. Then, I whip off the canvas. There stands the gleaming Gatling gun capable of delivering 360 rounds a minute. My hand resting lightly, confidently on the crank. They shall not pass, I say. Ils ne passeront pas. Then, the porcupine hide begins to fly.

I wonder if these rounds are still good?

•

The gigantic Gatling gun loomed over the herd like an immense piece of bad news.

"Hey Griswold."

"What?"

"He's got a gun."

"I *see* it," Griswold said. "You think I'm blind?"

"What we gonna do?"

"How about vamoose-ing?"

"But the herd . . ."

"Them li'l porcupines can take care of their own selves," Griswold said. "Goddamn it, I guess we better parley." He got up off the grass, where he had been stretched full-length, and walked toward the wagon.

"What say potner?"

"Look," the Dean said. "You can't enroll those porcupines. It's out of the question."

"That so?"

"It's out of the question," the Dean repeated. "We've

had a lot of trouble around here. The cops won't even speak to me. We can't *take* any more trouble." The Dean glanced at the herd. "That's a mighty handsome herd you have there."

"Kind of you," Griswold said. "That's a mighty handsome mule *you* got."

They both gazed at the Dean's terrible-looking mule.

Griswold wiped his neck with a red bandanna. "You don't want no porky-pines over to your place, is that it?"

"That's it."

"Well, we don't *go* where we ain't wanted," the wrangler said. "No call to throw down on us with that . . . *machine* there."

The Dean looked embarrassed.

"You don't know Mr. Sonny Bono, do you?" Griswold asked. "He lives around here somewheres, don't he?"

"I haven't had the pleasure," the Dean said. He thought for a moment. "I know a booker in Vegas, though. He was one of our people. He was a grad student in comparative religion."

"Maybe we can do a deal," the wrangler said. "Whichaway is New York City?"

•

"Well?" the Dean's wife asked. "What were their demands?"

"I'll tell you in a minute," the Dean said. "My mule is double-parked."

•

The herd turned onto the Cross Bronx Expressway. People looking out of their cars saw thousands and thousands of porcupines. The porcupines looked like badly engineered vacuum-cleaner attachments.

Vegas, the wrangler was thinking. Ten weeks at Caesar's Palace at a sock 15 G's a week. The Ballad of the Last Drive. Leroy Griswold singing his smash single, The Ballad of the Last Drive.

"Git along theah, li'l porcupines."

The citizens in their cars looked at the porcupines, thinking: What is wonderful? Are these porcupines wonderful? Are they significant? Are they what I need?

THE
EDUCATIONAL
EXPERIENCE

Music from somewhere. It is Vivaldi's great work, *The Semesters*.

The students wandered among the exhibits. The Fisher King was there. We walked among the industrial achievements. A good-looking gas turbine, behind a velvet rope. The manufacturers described themselves in their literature as "patient and optimistic." The students gazed, and gaped. Hitting them with ax handles is no longer permitted, hugging and kissing them is no longer permitted, speaking to them is permitted but only under extraordinary circumstances.

The Fisher King was there. In *Current Pathology* by Spurry and Entemann, the King is called "a doubtful clinical entity." But Spurry and Entemann have never caught him, so far as is known. Transfer of information from the world to the eye is permitted if you have signed oaths of loyalty to the world, to the eye, to *Current Pathology*.

We moved on. The two major theories of origin, evolution and creation, were argued by bands of believers who gave away buttons, balloons, bumper stickers, pieces of the True Cross. On the walls, photographs of stocking masks. The visible universe was doing very well, we decided, a great deal of movement, flux—unimpaired vitality. We made the students add odd figures, things like 453498*23:J and 8977?22MARY. This was part of the educational experience, we told them, and not even the hard part—just one side of a many-sided effort. But what a wonderful time you'll have, we told them, when the experience is over, done, completed. You will all, we told them, be more beautiful than you are now, and more employable too. You will have a grasp of the total situation; the total situation will have a grasp of you.

Here is a diode, learn what to do with it. Here is Du Guesclin, constable of France 1370–80—learn what to do with him. A divan is either a long cushioned seat or a council of state—figure out at which times it is what. Certainly you can have your dangerous drugs, but only for dessert—first you must chew your cauliflower, finish your fronds.

Oh they were happy going through the exercises and we told them to keep their tails down as they crawled under the wire, the wire was a string of quotations, Tacitus, Herodotus, Pindar . . . Then the steady-state cosmologists, Bondi, Gold, and Hoyle, had to be leaped over, the students had to swing from tree to tree in the Dark Wood, rappel down the sheer face of the Merzbau, engage in unarmed combat with the Van de Graaff machine, sew stocking masks. See? Unimpaired vitality.

We paused before a bird's lung on a pedestal. "But the mammalian lung is different!" they shouted. "A single slug of air, per hundred thousand population . . ." Some

126

fool was going to call for "action" soon, citing the su-
periority of praxis to pale theory. A wipe-out requires
thought, planning, coordination, as per our phoncon of
6/8/75. Classic film scripts were stretched tight over the
destruction of indigenous social and political structures
for dubious ends, as per our phoncon of 9/12/75. "Do
you think intelligent life exists outside this bed?" one student asked another, confused as to whether she was at-
tending the performance, or part of it. Unimpaired vitality, yes, but—

And Sergeant Preston of the Yukon was there in his
Sam Browne belt, he was copulating violently but copulating with no one, that's always sad to see. Still it was a
"nice try" and in that sense inspirational, a congratulation
to the visible universe for being what it is. The group
leader read from an approved text. "I have eaten from the
tympanum, I have drunk from the cymbals." The students
shouted and clashed their spears together, in approval.
We noticed that several of them were off in a corner playing with animals, an ibex, cattle, sheep. We didn't know
whether we should tell them to stop, or urge them to
continue. Perplexities of this kind are not infrequent in
our business. The important thing is the educational experience itself—how to survive it.

We moved them along as fast as we could, but it's difficult, with all the new regulations, restrictions. The Chapel
Perilous is a bomb farm now, they have eight thousand
acres in guavas and a few hundred head of white-faced
enlisted men who stand around with buckets of water,
buckets of sand. We weren't allowed to smoke, that was
annoying, but necessary I suppose to the preservation of
our fundamental ideals. Then we taught them how to put
stamps on letters, there was a long line waiting in front

of that part of the program, we lectured about belt buck-les, the off/on switch, and putting out the garbage. It is wise not to attempt too much all at once—perhaps we weren't wise.

The best way to live is by not knowing what will happen to you at the end of the day, when the sun goes down and the supper is to be cooked. The students looked at each other with secret smiles. Rotten of them to conceal their feelings from us, we who are doing the best we can. The invitation to indulge in emotion at the expense of rational analysis already constitutes a political act, as per our phoncon of 11/9/75. We came to a booth where the lessons of 1914 were taught. There were some wild straw-berries there, in the pool of blood, and someone was play-ing the piano, softly, in the pool of blood, and the Fisher King was fishing, hopelessly, in the pool of blood. The pool is a popular meeting place for younger people but we aren't younger any more so we hurried on. "Come and live with me," that was something somebody said to someone else, a bizarre idea that was quickly scotched—we don't want that kind of idea to become general, or popular.

"The world is everything that was formerly the case," the group leader said, "and now it is time to get back on the bus." Then all of the guards rushed up and demanded their bribes. We paid them with soluble traveler's checks and hoped for rain, and hoped for rodomontade, bragga-docio, blare, bray, fanfare, flourish, tucket.

THE DISCOVERY

"I'm depressed," Kate said.

Boots became worried. "Did I say something wrong?"

"You don't know *how* to say anything wrong."

"What?"

"The thing about you is, you're dull."

"I'm dull?"

There was a silence. Then Fog said: "Anybody want to go over to Springs to the rodeo?"

"Me?" Boots said. "Dull?"

The Judge got up and went over and sat down next to Kate.

"Now Kate, you oughtn't to be goin' round callin' Boots dull to his face. That's probably goin' to make him feel bad. I know you didn't mean it, really, and Boots knows it too, but he's gonna feel bad anyhow—"

"How 'bout the rodeo, over at Springs?" Fog asked again.

The Judge gazed sternly at his friend, Fog.

"—he's gonna feel bad, anyhow," the Judge continued, "just thinkin' you *mighta* meant it. So why don't you just tell him you didn't mean it."

"I did mean it."

"Aw come on, Katie. I know you mean what you say, but why make trouble? You can mean what you say, but why not say something else? On a nice day like this?"

The dry and lifeless air continued parching the concrete-like ground.

"It's not a nice day."

The Judge looked around. Then he said: "By God, Katie, you're right! It's a terrible day." Then he took a careful look at Boots, his son.

"I guess you think I'm dull, too, is that right, Pa?" Boots said with a disarming laugh.

"Well . . ."

Boots raised himself to his feet. He looked cool and unruffled, with just the hint of something in his eyes.

"So," he said. "So that's the way it is. So that's the way you, my own father, really feel about me. Well, it's a fine time to be sayin' something about it, wouldn't you say? In front of company and all?"

"Now don't get down on your old man," Fog said hastily. "Let's go to the rodeo."

"Fog—"

"He don't mean nothin' by it," Fog said. "He was just tryin' to tell the truth."

"Oh," Boots said. "He don't mean nothin' by it. He don't mean nothin' by it. Well, it seems to me I just been hearin' a lot of talk about people meanin' what they say. I am going to assume the Judge here means what he says."

"Yes," the Judge said. "I mean it."

"Yes," Kate said, "you have many fine qualities, Boots."

132

The Discovery

"See? He means it. My own father thinks I'm dull. And Katie thinks I'm dull. What about you, Fog? You want to make it unanimous?"

"Well Boots you are pretty doggone dull to my way of thinking. But nobody holds it against you. You got a lot of fine characteristics. Cain't everybody be Johnny Carson."

"Yes, there are lots duller than you, Boots," Kate said. "Harvey Brush, for example. Now that number is *really* dull."

"You're comparin' *me* with *Harvey Brush*?"

"Well I said he was worse, didn't I?"

"Good God."

"Why don't you go inside and read your letters from that girl in Brussels?" Kate suggested.

"*She* doesn't think I'm dull."

"Probably she don't understand English too good neither," the Judge said. "Now go on inside and read your mail or whatever. We just want to sit silently out here for a while."

"Goodbye."

After Boots had gone inside the Judge said: "My son."

"It is pretty terrible, Judge," Kate said.

"It's awful," Fog agreed.

"Well, it's not a hanging offense," the Judge said. "Maybe we can teach him some jokes or something."

"I've got to get back in the truck now," said Kate. "Judge, you have my deepest sympathy. If I can think of anything to do, I'll let you know."

"Thanks, Kate. It's always a pleasure to see you and be with you, wherever you are. *You* are never dull."

"I know that, Judge. Well, I'll see you later."

"O.K. Kate," said Fog. "Goodbye. Drive carefully."

"Goodbye Fog. Yes, I'll be careful."

133

"See you around, Kate."

"O.K., Judge. Goodbye, Fog."

"So long, Kate."

"See you. You know I can't marry that boy now, Judge. Knowing what I know."

"I understand, Kate. I wouldn't expect you to. I'll just have to dig up somebody else."

"It's going to be hard."

"Well, it's not going to be easy."

"So long, Kate," said Fog.

"O.K., goodbye. Be good."

"Yes," said Fog. "I'll try."

" 'Bye now, Judge."

"O.K., Katie."

"Wonder how come I never noticed it before?"

"Well don't *dwell* on it, Kate. See you in town."

"O.K., *adios.*"

"Goodbye, Kate."

"It's terrible but we've got it into focus now, haven't we?"

"I'm afraid we do."

"I sure would like to be of help, Judge."

"I know you would, Katie, and I appreciate it. I just don't see what can be done about it, right off."

"It's just his nature, probably."

"You're probably right. *I* was never dull."

"I know you weren't, Judge. Nobody blames you."

"Well, it's a problem."

"Quite a thorny one. But he'll be O.K., Judge. He's a good boy, basically."

"I know that, Kate. Well, we'll just have to wrestle with it."

"O.K., Judge. I'll see you later, O.K.?"

"Right."

"Behave yourself, Fog."

"Right, Katie."

"I'll see y'all. Bye-bye."

"Goodbye, Kate."

"You all right, Judge?"

"I'm fine, Katie. Just a little taken aback by what we've found out here today."

"Oh. O.K. Well, take care of yourself. You too, Fog."

"I will, Kate."

"O.K. See you two."

"Goodbye, Kate."

"You sure you don't want to come into town with me? I'll make you some tamale pie."

"That's O.K. Kate we got lots of stuff to eat right here."

"Oh. O.K. 'Bye."

The truck moved off into the dust.

"Look!" said the Judge. "She's waving."

"Wave back to her," Fog said.

"I am," said the Judge. "Look, I'm waving."

"I see it," said Fog. "Can she see you?"

"Maybe if I stand up," the Judge said. "Do you think she can see me now?"

"Not if she's watchin' the road."

"She's too young for us," the Judge said. He stopped waving.

"Depends on how you look at it," said Fog. "You want to go on over to the rodeo now?"

"I don't want to go to no rodeo," said the Judge. "All that youth."

REBECCA

Rebecca Lizard was trying to change her ugly, reptilian, thoroughly unacceptable last name.

"Lizard," said the judge. "Lizard, Lizard, Lizard. Lizard. There's nothing wrong with it if you say it enough times. You can't clutter up the court's calendar with trivial little minor irritations. And there have been far too many people changing their names lately. Changing your name countervails the best interests of the telephone company, the electric company, and the United States government. Motion denied."

Lizard in tears.

Lizard led from the courtroom. A chrysanthemum of Kleenex held under her nose.

"Shaky lady," said a man, "are you a schoolteacher?"

Of course she's a schoolteacher, you idiot. Can't you see the poor woman's all upset? Why don't you leave her alone?

"Are you a homosexual lesbian? Is that why you never married?"

Christ, yes, she's a homosexual lesbian, as you put it. *Would you please shut your face?*

Rebecca went to the damned dermatologist (a new damned dermatologist), but he said the same thing the others had said. "Greenish," he said, "slight greenishness, genetic anomaly, nothing to be done, I'm afraid, Mrs. Lizard."

"Miss Lizard."

"Nothing to be done, Miss Lizard."

"Thank you, Doctor. Can I give you a little something for your trouble?"

"Fifty dollars."

When Rebecca got home the retroactive rent increase was waiting for her, coiled in her mailbox like a pupil about to strike.

Must get some more Kleenex. Or a Ph.D. No other way.

She thought about sticking her head in the oven. But it was an electric oven.

Rebecca's lover, Hilda, came home late.

"How'd it go?" Hilda asked, referring to the day.

"Lousy."

"Hmm," Hilda said, and quietly mixed strong drinks of busthead for the two of them.

Hilda is a very good-looking woman. So is Rebecca. They love each other—an incredibly dangerous and delicate business, as we know. Hilda has long blond hair and is perhaps a shade the more beautiful. Of course Rebecca has a classic and sexual figure which attracts huge admiration from every beholder.

"You're late," Rebecca said. "Where were you?"

"I had a drink with Stephanie."

"Why did you have a drink with Stephanie?"

"She stopped by my office and said let's have a drink."

"Where did you go?"

"The Barclay."

"How is Stephanie?"

"She's fine."

"Why did you have to have a drink with Stephanie?"

"I was ready for a drink."

"Stephanie doesn't have a slight greenishness, is that it? Nice, pink Stephanie."

Hilda rose and put an excellent C. & W. album on the record-player. It was David Rogers's "Farewell to the Ryman," Atlantic SD 7283. It contains such favorites as "Blue Moon of Kentucky," "Great Speckled Bird," "I'm Movin' On," and "Walking the Floor over You." Many great Nashville personnel appear on this record.

"Pinkness is not everything," Hilda said. "And Stephanie is a little bit boring. You know that."

"Not so boring that you don't go out for drinks with her."

"I am not interested in Stephanie."

"As I was leaving the courthouse," Rebecca said, "a man unzipped my zipper."

David Rogers was singing "Oh please release me, let me go."

"What were you wearing?"

"What I'm wearing now."

"So he had good taste," Hilda said, "for a creep." She hugged Rebecca, on the sofa. "I love you," she said.

"Screw that," Rebecca said plainly, and pushed Hilda away. "Go hang out with Stephanie Sasser."

"I am not interested in Stephanie Sasser," Hilda said for the second time.

141

Very often one "pushes away" the very thing that one most wants to grab, like a lover. This is a common, although distressing, psychological mechanism, having to do (in my opinion) with the fact that what is presented is not presented "purely," that there is a tiny little canker or grim place in it somewhere. However, worse things can happen.

"Rebecca," said Hilda, "I really don't like your slight greenishness."

The term "lizard" also includes geckos, iguanas, chameleons, slowworms, and monitors. Twenty existing families make up the order, according to the *Larousse Encyclopedia of Animal Life,* and four others are known only from fossils. There are about twenty-five hundred species, and they display adaptations for walking, running, climbing, creeping, or burrowing. Many have interesting names, such as the Bearded Lizard, the Collared Lizard, the Flap-Footed Lizard, the Frilled Lizard, the Girdle-Tailed Lizard, and the Wall Lizard.

"I have been overlooking it for these several years, because I love you, but I really don't like it so much," Hilda said. "It's slightly—"

"Knew it," said Rebecca.

Rebecca went into the bedroom. The color-television set was turned on, for some reason. In a greenish glow, a film called *Green Hell* was unfolding.

I'm ill, I'm ill.

I will become a farmer.

Our love, our sexual love, our ordinary love!

Hilda entered the bedroom and said, "Supper is ready."

"What is it?"

"Pork with red cabbage."

"I'm drunk," Rebecca said.

Rebecca

Too many of our citizens are drunk at times when they should be sober—suppertime, for example. Drunkenness leads to forgetting where you have put your watch, keys, or money clip, and to a decreased sensitivity to the needs and desires and calm good health of others. The causes of overuse of alcohol are not as clear as the results. Psychiatrists feel in general that alcoholism is a serious problem but treatable, in some cases. A.A. is said to be both popular and effective. At base, the question is one of will power.

"Get up," Hilda said. "I'm sorry I said that."

"You told the truth," said Rebecca.

"Yes, it was the truth," Hilda admitted.

"You didn't tell me the truth in the beginning. In the beginning, you said it was beautiful."

"I was telling you the truth, in the beginning. I did think it was beautiful. Then."

This "then," the ultimate word in Hilda's series of three brief sentences, is one of the most pain-inducing words in the human vocabulary, when used in this sense. Departed time! And the former conditions that went with it! How is human pain to be measured? But remember that Hilda, too . . . It is correct to feel for Rebecca in this situation, but, reader, neither can Hilda's position be considered an enviable one, for truth, as Bergson knew, is a hard apple, whether one is throwing it or catching it.

"What remains?" Rebecca said stonily.

"I can love you *in spite of*—"

Do *I* want to be loved *in spite of*? Do you? Does anyone? But aren't we all, to some degree? Aren't there important parts of all of us which must be, so to say, gazed past? I turn a blind eye to that aspect of you, and you turn a blind eye to that aspect of me, and with these blind eyes eyeball-to-eyeball, to use an expression from the early 1960's, we continue our starched and fragrant lives. Of course it's also called "making the best of things," which I have always considered a rather soggy idea for an American ideal. But my criticisms of this idea must be tested against those of others—the late President McKinley, for example, who maintained that maintaining a good, if not necessarily sunny, disposition was the one valuable and proper course.

Hilda placed her hands on Rebecca's head.

"The snow is coming," she said. "Soon it will be snow time. Together then as in other snow times. Drinking busthead 'round the fire. Truth is a locked room that we knock the lock off from time to time, and then board up again. Tomorrow you will hurt me, and I will inform you that you have done so, and so on and so on. To hell with it. Come, viridian friend, come and sup with me."

They sit down together. The pork with red cabbage steams before them. They speak quietly about the McKinley Administration, which is being revised by revisionist historians. The story ends. It was written for several reasons. Nine of them are secrets. The tenth is that one should never cease considering human love. Which remains as grisly and golden as ever, no matter what is tattooed upon the warm tympanic page.

THE REFERENCE

"*Warp.*"

"In the character?"

"He warp *ever' which way.*"

"You don't think we should consider him, then."

"My friend Shel McPartland whom I have known deeply and intimately and too well for more than twenty years, is, sir, a brilliant O.K. engineer–master builder–cum–city and state planner. He'll plan your whole cotton-pickin' *state* for you, if you don't watch him. Right down to the flowers on the sideboard in the governor's mansion. He'll choose marginalia."

"I sir am not familiar sir with that particular bloom sir."

"Didn't think you would be, you bein' from Arkansas and therefore likely less than literate. You *are* the Arkansas State Planning Commission, are you not?"

"I am one of it. Mr. McPartland gave you as a reference."

147

"Well sir let me tell you sir that my friend Shel Mc-Partland who has incautiously put me down as a reference has a wide-ranging knowledge of all modern techniques, theories, dodges, orthodoxies, heresies, new and old innovations, and scams of all kinds. The only thing about him is, he warp."

"Sir, it is not necessary to use dialect when being telephone-called from the state of Arkansas."

"Different folk I talk to in different ways. I got to keep myself interested."

"I understand that. Leaving aside the question of warp for a minute, let me ask you this: Is Mr. McPartland what you would call a hard worker?"

"Hard, but warp. He sort of goes off in his own direction."

"Not a team player."

"Very much a team player. You get you your team out there, and he'll play it, and *beat* it, all by his own self."

"Does he fiddle with women?"

"No. He has too much love and respect for women. He has so much love and respect for women that he has nothing to do with them. At all."

"You said earlier that you wouldn't trust him to salt a mine shaft with silver dollars."

"Well sir that was before I fully understood the nature of your interest. I thought maybe you were thinking of going into *business* with him. Or some other damn-fool thing of that sort. Now that I understand that it's a government gig . . . You folks don't go around salting mine shafts with silver dollars, do you?"

"No sir, that work comes under the competence of the Arkansas Board of Earth Resources."

148

"So, not to worry."

"But it doesn't sound very likely if I may say so Mr. Cockburn sir that Mr. McPartland would neatly infit with our outfit. Which must of necessity as I'm sure you're hip to sir concern itself mostly with the mundanities."

"McPartland is sublime with the mundanities."

"Truly?"

"You should see him tying his shoes. Tying other people's shoes. He's good at inking-in. *Excellent* at erasing. One of the great erasers of our time. Plotting graphs. Figuring use-densities. Diddling flow charts. Inflating statistics. Issuing modestly deceptive reports. Chairing and charming. Dowsing for foundation funds. Only a fool and a simpleton sir would let a McPartland slip through his fingers."

"But before you twigged to the fact sir that your role was that of a referencer, you signaled grave and serious doubts."

"I have them still. I told you he was warp and he *is* warp. I am attempting dear friend to give you McPartland in the round. The whole man. The gravamen and the true gen. When we reference it up, here in the shop, we don't stint. Your interrobang meets our galgenspiel. We do good work."

"But is he reliable?"

"Reliability sir is much overrated. He is inspired. What does this lick pay, by the way?"

"In the low forties with perks."

"The perks include?"

"Arkansas air. Chauffeured VW to and from place of employment. Crab gumbo in the cafeteria every Tuesday. Ruffles and flourishes played on the Muzak upon entry and exit from building. Crab gumbo in the cafeteria every Thursday. Sabbaticals every second, third, and fifth year. Ox stoptions."

"The latter term is not known to me."

"Holder of the post is entitled to stop a runmad ox in the main street of Little Rock every Saturday at high noon, preventing thereby the mashing to strawberry yogurt of one small child furnished by management. Photograph of said act to appear in the local blats the following Sunday, along with awarding of medal by the mayor. On TV."

"Does the population never tire of this heroicidal behavior?"

"It's bread and circuitry in the modern world, sir, and no place in that world is more modern than Arkansas."

"Wherefrom do you get your crabs?"

"From our great sister state of Lose-e-anna, whereat the best world-class eating crabs hang out."

"The McPartland is a gumbohead from way back, this must be known to you from your other investigations."

"The organization is not to be tweedled with. Shelbaby's partialities will be catered to, if and when. Now I got a bunch more questions here. Like, is he good?"

"Good don't come close. One need only point to his accomplishments *in re* the sewer system of Detroit, Mich. By the sewage of Detroit I sat down and wept, from pure stunned admiration."

"Is he fake?"

"Not more than anybody else. He has façades but who does not?"

"Does he know the blue lines?"

"*Excellent* with the blue lines."

"Does he know the old songs?"

"He'll crack your heart with the old songs."

"Does he have the right moves?"

"People all over America are sitting in darkened projection rooms right this minute, studying the McPartland moves."

"What's this dude look like?"

"Handsome as the dawn. If you can imagine a bald dawn."

"You mean he's old?"

"Naw, man, he's young. A boy of forty-five, just like the rest of us. The thing is, he thinks so hard he done burned all the hair off his head. His head overheats."

"Is that a danger to standers-by?"

"Not if they exercise due caution. Don't stand too close."

"Maybe he's too fine for us."

"I don't think so. He's got a certain common-as-dirt quality. That's right under his laser-sharp M.I.T. quality."

"He sounds maybe a shade too rich for our blood. For us folk here in the downhome heartland."

"Lemme see, Arkansas, that's one of them newer states, right? Down there at the bottom edge? Right along with New Mexico and Florida and such as that?"

"Mr. Cockburn sir, are you jiving me?"

"Would I jive you?"

"Just for the record, how would you describe your personal relation to Mr. McPartland?"

"Oh I think 'bloody enemy' might do it. Might come close. At the same time, I am forced to acknowledge merit. In whatever obscene form it chooses to take. McPartland worked on the kiss of death, did you know that? When he was young. Never did get it perfected but the theoretical studies were elegant, elegant. He's what you might call a engineer's engineer. He designed the artichoke that is all heart. You pay a bit of a premium for it but you don't have to do all that peeling."

"Some people like the peeling. The leaf-by-leaf unveiling."

"Well, some people like to bang their heads against stone walls, don't they? Some people like to sleep with their sisters. Some people like to put on suits and ties and go sit in a concert hall and listen to the New York Philharmonic *Orchestra* for God's sake. Some people—"

"Is this part of his warp?"

"It's related to his warp. The warp to power."

"Any other glaring defects or lesions of the usual that you'd like to touch upon—"

"I think not. Now you, I perceive, have got this bad situation down there in the great state of Arkansas. Your population is exploding. It's mobile. You got people moving freely about, colliding and colluding, pairing off just as they please and exploding the population some more, lollygagging and sailboating and making leather moccasins from kits and God knows what all. And enjoying free speech and voting their heads off and vetoing bond issues carefully thought up and packaged and rigged by the Arkansas State Planning Commission. And generally helter-skeltering around under the gross equity of the democratic system. Is that the position, sir?"

"Worse. Arkansas is, at present, pure planarchy."

"I intuited as much. And you need someone who can get the troops back on the track or tracks. Give them multifamily dwellings, green belts, dayrooms, grog rations, and pleasure stamps. Return the great state of Arkansas to its originary tidiness. Exert a planipotentiary beneficence while remaining a masked marvel. Whose very existence is known only to the choice few."

"Exactly right. Can McPartland do it?"

"Sitting on his hands. Will you go to fifty?"

"Fervently and with pleasure, sir. It's little enough for such a treasure."

"I take 10 percent off the top, sir."

"And can I send you as well, sir, a crate of armadillo steaks, sugar-cured, courtesy of the A.S.P.C.? It's a dream of beauty, sir, this picture that you've limned."

"Not a dream, sir, not a dream. Engineers, sir, never sleep, and dream only in the daytime."

THE NEW
MEMBER

The presiding officer noted that there was a man standing outside the window looking in.

The members of the committee looked in the direction of the window and found that the presiding officer's observation was correct: There was a man standing outside the window looking in.

Mr. Macksey moved that the record take note of the fact.

Mr. O'Donoghue seconded. The motion passed.

Mrs. Brown wondered if someone should go out and talk to the man standing outside the window.

Mrs. Mallory suggested that the committee proceed as if the man standing outside the window wasn't there. Maybe he'd go away, she suggested.

Mr. Macksey said that that was an excellent idea and so moved.

Mr. O'Donoghue wondered if the matter required a motion.

The presiding officer ruled that the man standing outside the window looking in did not require a motion.

Ellen West said that she was frightened.

Mr. Birnbaum said there was nothing to be frightened about.

Ellen West said that the man standing outside the window looked larger than a man to her. Maybe it was not human, she said.

Mr. Macksey said that that was nonsense and that it was only just a very large man, probably.

The presiding officer stated that the committee had a number of pressing items on the agenda and wondered if the meeting could go forward.

Not with that thing out there, Ellen West said.

The presiding officer stated that the next order of business was the matter of the Worth girl.

Mr. Birnbaum noted that the Worth girl had been doing very well.

Mrs. Brown said quite a bit better than well, in her opinion.

Mr. O'Donoghue said that the improvement was quite remarkable.

The presiding officer noted that the field in which she, the Worth girl, was working was a very abstruse one and, moreover, one in which very few women had successfully established themselves.

Mrs. Brown said that she had known the girl's mother quite well and that she had been an extremely pleasant person.

Ellen West said that the man was still outside the window and hadn't moved.

Mr. O'Donoghue said that there was, of course, the possibility that the Worth girl was doing too well.

Mr. Birnbaum said there was such a thing as too much too soon.

Mr. Percy inquired as to the girl's age at the present time and was told she was thirty-five. He then said that that didn't sound like "too soon" to him.

The presiding officer asked for a motion.

Mr. O'Donoghue moved that the Worth girl be hit by a car.

Mr. Birnbaum seconded.

The presiding officer asked for discussion.

Mrs. Mallory asked if Mr. O'Donoghue meant fatally. Mr. O'Donoghue said he did.

Mr. Percy said he thought that a fatal accident, while consonant with the usual procedures of the committee, was always less interesting than something that left the person alive, so that the person's situation was still, in a way, "open."

Mr. O'Donoghue said that Mr. Percy's well-known liberalism was a constant source of strength and encouragement to every member of the committee, as was Mr. Percy's well-known predictability.

Mrs. Mallory said wouldn't it look like the committee was punishing excellence?

Mr. O'Donoghue said that a concern for how things looked was not and should never be a consideration of the committee.

Ellen West said that she thought the man standing outside the window looking in was listening. She reminded the committee that the committee's deliberations were supposed to be held *in camera*.

The presiding officer said that the man could not hear through the glass of the window.

Ellen West said was he sure?

The presiding officer asked if Ellen West would like to be put on some other committee.

Ellen West said that she only felt safe on this committee.

The presiding officer reminded her that even members of the committee were subject to the decisions of the committee, except of course for the presiding officer.

Ellen West said she realized that and would like to move that the Worth girl fall in love with somebody.

The presiding officer said that there was already a motion before the committee and asked if the committee was ready for a vote. The committee said it was. The motion was voted on and failed, 14–4.

Ellen West moved that the Worth girl fall in love with the man standing outside the window.

Mr. Macksey said you're just trying to get him inside so we can take a look at him.

Ellen West said well, why not, if you're so sure he's harmless.

The presiding officer said that he felt that if the man outside were invited inside, a confusion of zones would result, which would be improper.

Mr. Birnbaum said that it might not be a bad idea if the committee got a little feedback from the people for whom it was responsible, once in a while.

Mrs. Mallory stated that she thought Mr. Birnbaum's idea about feedback was a valuable and intelligent one but that she didn't approve of having such a warm and beautiful human being as the Worth girl fall in love with an unknown quantity with demonstrably peculiar habits, *vide* the window, just to provide feedback to the committee.

Mrs. Brown repeated that she had known the Worth girl's mother.

Mr. Macksey asked if Ellen West intended that the Worth girl's love affair be a happy or an unhappy one.

Ellen West said she would not wish to overdetermine somebody else's love affair.

Mr. O'Donoghue moved that the Worth girl be run over by a snowmobile.

The presiding officer said that O'Donoghue was out of order and also that in his judgment Mr. O'Donoghue was reintroducing a defeated motion in disguised form.

Mr. O'Donoghue said that he could introduce new motions all night long, if he so chose.

Mrs. Brown said that she had to be home by ten to receive a long-distance phone call from her daughter in Oregon.

The presiding officer said that as there was no second, Ellen West's motion about the man outside the window need not be discussed further. He suggested that as there were four additional cases awaiting disposition by the committee he wondered if the case of the Worth girl, which was after all not that urgent, might not be tabled until the next meeting.

Mr. Macksey asked what were the additional cases.

The presiding officer said those of Dr. Benjamin Pierce, Casey McManus, Cynthia Croneis, and Ralph Lorant.

Mr. Percy said that those were not very interesting names. To him.

Mr. Macksey moved that the Worth girl be tabled. Mr. Birnbaum seconded. The motion carried.

Mr. Birnbaum asked if he might have a moment for a general observation bearing on the work of the committee. The presiding officer graciously assented.

AMATEURS

Mr. Birnbaum said that he had observed, in the ordinary course of going around taking care of his business and so on, that there were not many pregnant women now. He said that yesterday he had seen an obviously pregnant woman waiting for a bus and had remembered that in the last half year he had seen no others. He said he wondered why this was and whether it wasn't within the purview of the committee that there be more pregnant women, for the general good of the community, to say nothing of the future.

Mrs. Mallory said she knew why it was.

Mr. Birnbaum said why? and Mrs. Mallory smiled enigmatically.

Mr. Birnbaum repeated his question and Mrs. Mallory smiled enigmatically again.

Oh me oh my, said Mr. Birnbaum.

The presiding officer said that Mr. Birnbaum's observations, as amplified in a sense by Mrs. Mallory, were of considerable interest.

He said further that such matters were a legitimate concern of the committee and that if he might be allowed to speak for a moment not as the presiding officer but merely as an ordinary member of the committee he would urge, strongly urge, that Cynthia Croneis become pregnant immediately and that she should have twin boys.

Hear hear, said Mr. Macksey.

How about a boy and a girl? asked Ellen West.

The presiding officer said that would be O.K. with him.

This was moved, seconded, and voted unanimously.

On Mr. Macksey's motion it was decided that Dr. Pierce win fifty thousand dollars in the lottery.

It was pointed out by Mrs. Brown that Dr. Pierce was already quite well fixed, financially.

The New Member

The presiding officer reminded the members that justice was not a concern of the committee.

On Mr. Percy's motion it was decided that Casey McManus would pass the Graduate Record Examination with a score in the upper 10 percent. On Mr. O'Donoghue's motion it was decided that Ralph Lorant would have his leg broken by having it run over by a snowmobile.

Mr. Birnbaum looked at the window and said he's still out there.

Mr. O'Donoghue said for God's sake, let's have him in.

Mr. Macksey went outside and asked the man in.

The man hesitated in the doorway for a moment.

Mr. Percy said come in, come in, don't be nervous.

The presiding officer added his urgings to Mr. Percy's.

The man left the doorway and stood in the middle of the room.

The presiding officer inquired if the man had, perhaps, a grievance he wished to bring to the attention of the committee.

The man said no, no grievance.

Why then was he standing outside the window looking in? Mr. Macksey asked.

The man said something about just wanting to "be with somebody."

Mr. Percy asked if he had a family, and the man said no.

Are you from around here? asked Mrs. Mallory, and the man shook his head.

Employed? asked Mr. Birnbaum, and the man shook his head.

He wants to be with somebody, Mrs. Mallory said.

Yes, said the presiding officer, I understand that.

It's not unusual, said Mr. Macksey.

Not unusual at all, said Mrs. Brown. She again reminded the members that she had to be home by ten to receive a call from her daughter in Oregon.

Maybe we should make him a member of the committee, said Mr. Percy.

He could give us some feedback, said Mr. Birnbaum. I mean, I would assume that.

Ellen West moved that the man be made a member of the committee. Mr. Birnbaum seconded. The motion was passed, 12–6.

Mr. Percy got up and got a folding chair for the man and pulled it up to the committee table.

The man sat down in the chair and pulled it closer to the table.

All right, he said. The first thing we'll do is, we'll make everybody wear overalls. Gray overalls. Gray overalls with gray T-shirts. We'll have morning prayers, evening prayers, and lunch prayers. Calisthenics for everyone over the age of four in the 5–7 p.m. time slot. Boutonnieres are forbidden. Nose rings are forbidden. Gatherings of one or more persons are prohibited. On the question of bedtime, I am of two minds.

YOU ARE
AS BRAVE
AS VINCENT
VAN GOGH

You eavesdrop in three languages. Has no one ever told you not to pet a leashed dog? We wash your bloody hand with Scotch from the restaurant.

Children. *I want one,* you say, pointing to a mother pushing a pram. And there's not much time. But the immense road-mending machine (yellow) cannot have children, even though it is a member of a family, it has siblings—the sheep's-foot roller, the air hammer.

You ask: Will there be fireworks?

I would never pour lye in your eyes, you say.

Where do you draw the line? I ask. Top Job?

Shall we take a walk? Is there a trout stream? Can one rent a car? Is there dancing? Sailing? Dope? Do you know Saint-Exupéry? Wind? Sand? Stars? Night flight?

You don't offer to cook dinner for me again today.

The air hammer with the miserable sweating workman hanging on to the handles. I assimilated the sexual significance of the air hammer long ago. It's new to you. You are too young.

You move toward the pool in your black bikini, you will open people's pop-top Pepsis for them, explicate the Torah, lave the brown shoulders of new acquaintances with Bain de Soleil.

You kick me in the backs of the legs while I sleep.

You are staring at James. James is staring back. There are six of us sitting on the floor around a low, glass-topped table. I become angry. Is there no end to it?

See, there is a boy opening a fire hydrant, you stand closer, see, he has a large wrench on top of the hydrant and he is turning the wrench, the water rushes from the hydrant, you bend to feel the water on your hand.

You are reading *From Ritual to Romance*, by Jessie L. Weston. But others have read it before you. Practically everyone has read it.

At the pool, you read Saint-Exupéry. But wait, there is a yellow nylon cord crossing the pool, yellow nylon supported by red-and-blue plastic floats, it divides the children's part from the deeper part, you are in the pool investigating, flexing the nylon cord, pulling on it, yes, it is firmly attached to the side of the pool, to both sides of the pool. And in the kitchen you regard the salad chef, a handsome young Frenchman, he stares at you, at your tanned breasts, at your long dark (wet) hair, can one, would it be possible, at this hour, a cup of coffee, or perhaps tea . . .

Soon you will be thirty.

And the giant piece of yellow road-mending equipment enters the pool, silently, you are in the cab, manipulating the gears, levers, shove this one forward and the machine swims. Swims toward the man in the Day-Glo orange vest who is waving his Day-Glo orange flags in the air, this way, this way, here!

He's a saint, you say. Did you ever try to live with a saint?

You telephone to tell me you love me before going out to do something I don't want you to do.

If you are not asking for fireworks you are asking for Miles Davis bound hand and foot, or Iceland. You make no small plans.

See, there is a blue BOAC flight bag, open, on the floor, inside it a folded newspaper, a towel, and something wrapped in silver foil. You bend over the flight bag (whose is it? you don't know) and begin to unwrap the object wrapped in silver foil. Half a loaf of bread. Satisfied, you wrap it up again.

You return from California too late to vote. One minute too late. I went across the street to the school with you. They had locked the doors. I remember your banging on the doors. No one came to open them. Tears. *What difference does one minute make?* you screamed, in the direction of the doors.

Your husband, you say, is a saint.

And did no one ever tell you that the staircase you climbed in your dream, carrying the long brown velvet skirt, in your dream, is a very old staircase?

I remind myself to tell you that you are abnormally intelligent. You kick me in the backs of the legs again, while I sleep.

Parades, balloons, fêtes, horse races.

You feel your time is limited. Tomorrow, you think, there will be three deep creases in your forehead. You offer to quit your job, if that would please me. I say that you cannot quit your job, because you are abnormally intelligent. Your job needs you.

The salad chef moves in your direction, but you are lying on your back on the tennis court, parallel with and under the net, turning your head this way and that, applauding the players, one a tall man with a rump as big as his belly, which is huge, the other a fourteen-year-old girl, intent, lean stringy hair, sorry, good shot, nice one, your sunglasses stuck in your hair. You rush toward the mountain which is furnished with trees, ski lifts, power lines, deck chairs, wedding invitations, you invade the mountain as if it were a book, leaping into the middle, checking the ending, ignoring the beginning. And look there, a locked door! You try the handle, first lightly, then viciously.

You once left your open umbrella outside the A&P, tied to the store with a string. When you came out of the store with your packages, you were surprised to find it gone.

The three buildings across the street from my apartment—one red, one yellow, one brown—are like a Hopper in the slanting late-afternoon light. See? Like a Hopper.

Is that a rash on my chest? Between the breasts? Those little white marks? Look, those people at the next table, all have ordered escargots, seven dozen in garlic butter arriving all at once, eighty-four dead snails on a single surface, in garlic butter. And last night, when it was so hot, I opened the doors to the balcony, I couldn't sleep, I lay awake, I thought I heard something, I imagined someone climbing over the balcony, I got up to see but there was no one.

You are as beautiful as twelve Hoppers.

You are as brave as Vincent van Gogh.

You Are as Brave as Vincent van Gogh

I make fireworks for you:
!!]*!!*[!*!* and *%%*+&+&+*%%*.
If he is a saint, why did you marry him? It makes no
sense. Outside in the street, some men with a cherry
picker are placing new high-intensity bulbs in all the
street lights, so that our criminals will be scalded, trans-
figured with light.
Yesterday you asked me for the Princeton University
Press.
The Princeton University Press is not a toy, I said.
It's not?
And then: Can we go to a *movie* in which there are
fireworks?
But there are fireworks in all movies, that is what
movies are for—what they do for us.
You should not have left the baby on the lawn. In a
hailstorm. When we brought him inside, he was covered
with dime-size blue bruises.

AT THE END
OF THE
MECHANICAL
AGE

I went to the grocery store to buy some soap. I stood for a long time before the soaps in their attractive boxes, RUB and FAB and TUB and suchlike, I couldn't decide so I closed my eyes and reached out blindly and when I opened my eyes I found her hand in mine.

Her name was Mrs. Davis, she said, and TUB was best for important cleaning experiences, in her opinion. So we went to lunch at a Mexican restaurant which as it happened she owned, she took me into the kitchen and showed me her stacks of handsome beige tortillas and the steam tables which were shiny-brite. I told her I wasn't very good with women and she said it didn't matter, few men were, and that nothing mattered, now that Jake was gone, but I would do as an interim project and sit down and have a Carta Blanca. So I sat down and had a cool Carta Blanca, God was standing in the basement reading the meters to see how much grace had been used up in the month of June. Grace is electricity, science has found, it

175

is not *like* electricity, it *is* electricity and God was down in the basement reading the meters in His blue jump suit with the flashlight stuck in the back pocket.

"The mechanical age is drawing to a close," I said to her.

"Or has already done so," she replied.

"It was a good age," I said. "I was comfortable in it, relatively. Probably I will not enjoy the age to come quite so much. I don't like its look."

"One must be fair. We don't know yet what kind of an age the next one will be. Although I feel in my bones that it will be an age inimical to personal well-being and comfort, and that is what I like, personal well-being and comfort."

"Do you suppose there is something to be done?" I asked her.

"Huddle and cling," said Mrs. Davis. "We can huddle and cling. It will pall, of course, everything palls, in time . . ."

Then we went back to my house to huddle and cling, most women are two different colors when they remove their clothes especially in summer but Mrs. Davis was all one color, an ocher. She seemed to like huddling and clinging, she stayed for many days. From time to time she checked the restaurant keeping everything shiny-brite and distributing sums of money to the staff, returning with tortillas in sacks, cases of Carta Blanca, buckets of guacamole, but I paid her for it because I didn't want to feel obligated.

There was a song I sang her, a song of great expectations.

"*Ralph is coming,*" I sang, "*Ralph is striding in his suit of lights over moons and mountains, over parking lots and*

*fountains, toward your silky side. Ralph is coming, he has
a coat of many colors and all major credit cards and he is
striding to meet you and culminate your foggy dreams in
an explosion of blood and soil, at the end of the mechanical age. Ralph is coming preceded by fifty running men
with spears and fifty dancing ladies who are throwing leaf
spinach out of little baskets, in his path. Ralph is perfect,"*
I sang, *"but he is also full of interesting tragic flaws, and
he can drink fifty running men under the table without
breaking his stride and he can have congress with fifty
dancing ladies without breaking his stride, even his socks
are ironed, so natty is Ralph, but he is also right down in
the mud with the rest of us, he markets the mud at high
prices for specialized industrial uses and he is striding,
striding, striding, toward your waiting heart. Of course
you may not like him, some people are awfully picky . . .
Ralph is coming,"* I sang to her, *"he is striding over dap-
pled plains and crazy rivers and he will change your life
for the better, probably, you will be fainting with glee at
the simple touch of his grave gentle immense hand although I am aware that some people can't stand pros-
perity, Ralph is coming, I hear his hoofsteps on the drum-
head of history, he is striding as he has been all his life
toward you, you, you."*

"Yes," Mrs. Davis said, when I had finished singing,
"that is what I deserve, all right. But probably I will not
get it. And in the meantime, there is you."

.

God then rained for forty days and forty nights, when
the water tore away the front of the house we got into

the boat, Mrs. Davis liked the way I maneuvered the boat off the trailer and out of the garage, she was provoked into a memoir of Jake.

"Jake was a straight-ahead kind of man," she said, "he was simpleminded and that helped him to be the kind of man that he was." She was staring into her Scotch-and-floodwater rather moodily I thought, debris bouncing on the waves all around us but she paid no attention. "That is the type of man I like," she said, "a strong and simpleminded man. The case-study method was not Jake's method, he went right through the middle of the line and never failed to gain yardage, no matter what the game was. He had a lust for life, and life had a lust for him. I was inconsolable when Jake passed away." Mrs. Davis was drinking the Scotch for her nerves, she had no nerves of course, she was nerveless and possibly heartless also but that is another question, gutless she was not, she had a gut and a very pretty one ocher in color but that was another matter. God was standing up to His neck in the raging waters with a smile of incredible beauty on His visage, He seemed to be enjoying His creation, the disaster, the waters all around us were raging louder now, raging like a mighty tractor-trailer tailgating you on the highway.

Then Mrs. Davis sang to me, a song of great expectations.

"*Maude is waiting for you,*" Mrs. Davis sang to me, "*Maude is waiting for you in all her seriousness and splendor, under her gilded onion dome, in that city which I cannot name at this time, Maude waits. Maude is what you lack, the profoundest of your lacks. Your every yearn since the first yearn has been a yearn for Maude, only you did not know it until I, your dear friend, pointed it out.*

178

At the End of the Mechanical Age

She is going to heal your scrappy and generally unsatis-
factory life with the balm of her Maudeness, luckiest of
dogs, she waits only for you. Let me give you just one
instance of Maude's inhuman sagacity. Maude named the
tools. It was Maude who thought of calling the rattail file
a rattail file. It was Maude who christened the needle-nose
pliers. Maude named the rasp. Think of it. What else
could a rasp be but a rasp? Maude in her wisdom went
right to the point, and called it rasp. *It was Maude who*
named the maul. Similarly the sledge, the wedge, the ball-
peen hammer, the adz, the shim, the hone, the strop. The
handsaw, the hacksaw, the bucksaw, and the fretsaw
were named by Maude, peering into each saw and intuit-
ing at once its specialness. The scratch awl, the scuffle
hoe, the prick punch and the countersink—I could go on
and on. The tools came to Maude, tool by tool in a long
respectful line, she gave them their names. The vise. The
gimlet. The cold chisel. The reamer, the router, the gouge.
The plumb bob. How could she have thought up the rough
justice of these wonderful cognomens? Looking languidly
at a pair of tin snips, and then deciding to call them tin
snips—*what a burst of glory! And I haven't even cited the*
bush hook, the grass snath, or the plumber's snake, or the
C-clamp, or the nippers, or the scythe. What a tall achieve-
ment, naming the tools! And this is just one of Maude's
contributions to our worldly estate, there are others. What
delights will come crowding," Mrs. Davis sang to me, *"de-*
light upon delight, when the epithalamium is ground out
by the hundred organ grinders who are Maude's constant
attendants, on that good-quality day of her own choosing,
which you have desperately desired all your lean life, only
you weren't aware of it until I, your dear friend, pointed it
out. And Maude is young but not too young," Mrs. Davis

sang to me, *"she is not too old either, she is* just right *and she is waiting for you with her tawny limbs and horse sense, when you receive Maude's nod your future and your past will begin."*

There was a pause, or pall.

"Is that true," I asked, "that song?"

"It is a metaphor," said Mrs. Davis, "it has metaphorical truth."

"And the end of the mechanical age," I said, "is that a metaphor?"

"The end of the mechanical age," said Mrs. Davis, "is in my judgment an actuality straining to become a metaphor. One must wish it luck, I suppose. One must cheer it on. Intellectual rigor demands that we give these damned metaphors every chance, even if they are inimical to personal well-being and comfort. We have a duty to understand everything, whether we like it or not—a duty I would scant if I could." At that moment the water jumped into the boat and sank us.

•

At the wedding Mrs. Davis spoke to me kindly.

"Tom," she said, "you are not Ralph, but you are all that is around at the moment. I have taken in the whole horizon with a single sweep of my practiced eye, no giant figure looms there and that is why I have decided to marry you, temporarily, with Jake gone and an age ending. It will be a marriage of convenience all right, and when Ralph comes, or Maude nods, then our arrangement will automatically self-destruct, like the tinted bubble that it is. You were very kind and considerate, when we were drying out, in the tree, and I appreciated that. That counted for something. Of course kindness and consideration are not what the great songs, the Ralph-song and the Maude-song, promise. They are merely flaky substitutes for the terminal experience. I realize that and want you to realize it. I want to be straight with you. That is one of the most admirable things about me, that I am always straight with people, from the sweet beginning to the bitter end. Now I will return to the big house where my handmaidens will proceed with the robing of the bride."

It was cool in the meadow by the river, the meadow Mrs. Davis had selected for the travesty, I walked over to the tree under which my friend Blackie was standing, he was the best man, in a sense.

"This disgusts me," Blackie said, "this hollow pretense and empty sham and I had to come all the way from Chicago."

God came to the wedding and stood behind a tree with just part of His effulgence showing, I wondered whether He was planning to bless this makeshift construct with His grace, or not. It's hard to imagine what He was thinking of in the beginning when He planned everything that was ever going to happen, planned everything exquisitely right down to the tiniest detail such as what I was thinking at this very moment, my thought about His thought, planned the end of the mechanical age and detailed the new age to follow, and then the bride emerged from the house with her train, all ocher in color and very lovely.

"And do you, Anne," the minister said, "promise to make whatever mutually satisfactory accommodations necessary to reduce tensions and arrive at whatever previously agreed-upon goals both parties have harmoniously set in the appropriate planning sessions?"

"I do," said Mrs. Davis.

"And do you, Thomas, promise to explore all differences thoroughly with patience and inner honesty ignoring no fruitful avenues of discussion and seeking at all times to achieve rapprochement while eschewing advantage in conflict situations?"

"Yes," I said.

"Well, now we are married," said Mrs. Davis, "I think I will retain my present name if you don't mind, I have always been Mrs. Davis and your name is a shade graceless, no offense, dear."

"O.K.," I said.

Then we received the congratulations and good wishes of the guests, who were mostly employees of the Mexican restaurant, Raul was there and Consuelo, Pedro, and Pepe came crowding around with outstretched hands and Blackie came crowding around with outstretched hands, God was standing behind the caterer's tables looking at the enchiladas and chalupas and chile con queso and chicken mole as if He had never seen such things before but that was hard to believe.

I started to speak to Him as all of the world's great religions with a few exceptions urge, from the heart, I started to say "Lord, Little Father of the Poor, and all that, I was just wondering now that an age, the mechanical age, is ending and a new age beginning or so they say, I was just wondering if You could give me a hint, sort of, not a Sign, I'm not asking for a Sign, but just the barest hint as to whether what we have been told about Your nature and our nature is, forgive me and I know how You feel about doubt or rather what we have been told You feel about it, but if You could just let drop the slightest indication as to whether what we have been told is authentic or just a bunch of apocryphal heterodoxy—"

But He had gone away with an insanely beautiful smile on His lighted countenance, gone away to read the meters and get a line on the efficacy of grace in that area, I surmised, I couldn't blame Him, my question had not been so very elegantly put, had I been able to express it mathematically He would have been more interested, maybe, but I have never been able to express anything mathematically.

After the marriage Mrs. Davis explained marriage to me.

Marriage, she said, an institution deeply enmeshed with the mechanical age.

Pairings smiled upon by law were but reifications of the laws of mechanics, inspired by unions of a technical nature, such as nut with bolt, wood with wood screw, aircraft with Plane-Mate.

Permanence or impermanence of the bond a function of (1) materials and (2) technique.

Growth of literacy a factor, she said.

Growth of illiteracy also.

The center will not hold if it has been spot-welded by an operator whose deepest concern is not with the weld but with his lottery ticket.

God interested only in grace—keeping things humming.

Blackouts, brownouts, temporary dimmings of household illumination all portents not of Divine displeasure but of Divine indifference to executive-development programs at middle-management levels.

He likes to get out into the field Himself, she said. With His flashlight. He is doing the best He can.

We two, she and I, no exception to general ebb/flow of world juice and its concomitant psychological effects, she said.

Bitter with the sweet, she said.

•

After the explanation came the divorce.

"Will you be wanting to contest the divorce?" I asked Mrs. Davis.

"I think not," she said calmly, "although I suppose one of us should, for the fun of the thing. An uncontested divorce always seems to me contrary to the spirit of divorce."

"That is true," I said, "I have had the same feeling myself, not infrequently."

After the divorce the child was born. We named him A.F. of L. Davis and sent him to that part of Russia where people live to be one hundred and ten years old. He is living there still, probably, growing in wisdom and beauty. Then we shook hands, Mrs. Davis and I, and she set out Ralphward, and I, Maudeward, the glow of hope not yet extinguished, the fear of pall not yet triumphant, standby generators ensuring the flow of grace to all of God's creatures at the end of the mechanical age.